*"Reality exists in the human mind,
and nowhere else."*

— George Orwell

OVER
CORAL ISLAND

NICK POWER

Illustrations by Ian Skelly

Words by Nick Power
Illustrations by Ian Skelly
Poem in 'Poem on the Alleyway Floor' by James Skelly
'Finniland Song of the Lightning Tree' score by Bill Ryder-Jones
Cover design by Side Show Hustle Inc.
Book design by Conor Moore
Copyright © 2020 Power / Skelly
All rights reserved.

Published by Murdered Crow Press
Printed by Book Printing UK www.bookprintinguk.com
Remus House, Coltsfoot Drive, Peterborough, PE2 9BF

Printed in Great Britain

CONTENTS

Over Coral Island

The Dips 5

She Owns Acres 11

Luna the Fire Eater 17

First Night of the Holidays 23

Downhome Special 25

So That I Dream No More 33

The Werewolf 45

Coral Island Picture House 49

After the Closure of Coral Island Picture House 51

Letter to Shannon 53

Holy Joe 63

Poem on the Alleyway Floor 69

The Great Lafayette 73

Fourth Night of the Holidays 77

The Mating Call of a Fox 79

Not For Sale 81

Muriel & Miranda (The Mermaid Twins) 93

Over Coral Island 97

The Visitors 101

The Lightning Tree 109

Running with the Dogs 125

Jono 131

Jody and the Kid 135

Prophet Zaar and the Happiness Machine 145

Less Than Nothing 151

It Wasn't Always Like This 153

Snake Mountain Rollercoaster 155

Circus Drivers 159

Holes 165

Local Focus 167

The Coral Island Steeplechase Disaster 169

Last Night of the Holidays 175

The Light the Dead See 177

Why The Arklow Caught Fire at Coral Bay 181

Last Night of the Fair 183

OVER
CORAL ISLAND

THE DIPS

Jono says I can't do it.

Jono says I'll never be able to do it because I can't get the rhythm.

Jono says to get away from the barrier when he turns it full speed because if I go under I'll come out a mixed kebab.

It'll be so bad, he says, even the butchers won't want me.

And I don't want to be in the dog's belly, no one does.

We always arrive at night. I know we're coming into The Dips or the fields or the farmland because the traction on the tyres goes from smooth to squishy and you can hear the mud gurgling in the treads and in the morning the moocows are outside chewing the cud.

We can set up anywhere on the island so long as it's not near the piers because then the man with the briefcase comes and Jono says he can't fight the man with the briefcase.

Jono is last to bed and first up in the mornings, out there hammering the tent pegs, three men at a time, Jono, Kip and Tiny the giant. The hammers go up like swinging pendulum machines, heave-ho, clink, one-two-three, and they're back weightless then, soaring over Jono's shoulder like wood pigeons before falling again.

5

After the big top goes up Jono comes to the trailer, drinks coffee and gets Dad out of bed. Dad sits outside in a deckchair all day. He doesn't talk any more. He just sits there smoking, a tube up each of his nostrils that go to a silver oxygen cylinder.

When he breathes in he sounds like an old door and when he breathes out it's like bombs going off.

His skin is the colour of air.

Once Jono has fed Dad, he goes to the back and unpacks the big satellite dish, wiring it up to the battery of the van and pointing it toward space like a flying saucer waiting to take off.

Me and my brother Connie will be up by then, surfing through channels on the long couch, one big quilt over us, waiting for the UFC or wrestling to start.

Jono brings us cereal in bowls. He smells like a car engine.

When the night comes back, everything is different. If we're near the North Pier, Connie and me will hitchhike up to play the bandits or the virtual horse racing. If we're in the middle of nowhere, we'll wander around our fair and drink in its strangled magic.

Everything is lit up. Tents heave with people. Carousels spin. The whoosh of the biggest ride, The Mist on the River, is followed by the scream of frightened passengers as it loops the loop around the hangman's bluff.

Jono does the waltzers while we watch. It's like a

dance, how he does it.

God, you should see him.

It starts off slow-like, and Jono is in the paybox. He's talking on the muffled microphone. The people are barred in by now and the waltzers get going. *Here we go, merry-we-go-round.*

Jono comes out of the paybox. There's a song on the Tannoy called Downbound Train, and it moves and skips as the waltzers speed up.

He jumps to the static platform in middle, dodging the moving cars as the undulating floor rises and falls and then everything is spinning.

Hands in the air.

You can hear noises - squeals, groans and laughter. They get louder as the ride accelerates.

Jono becomes light as a feather. He ghosts in between the cars, spinning and pushing, each one coming at him like spitfire bullets.

He knows where to go.

He drops his hip once, jumps forward, spins one car behind him with a back kick and spins the other in front with a flick of his leading hand. All of this with a ciggy in his gob.

The girls are watching too, lined up on the long wall in front of the punch bag machines.

Jono won't look over because of Tammy.

Tammy is the one he's got four pictures of in the cab of the truck where he sleeps. They're stuck above his bunk in the shape of the Holy Cross.

When the carousel is spinning full speed, Jono is moving so fast I swear it looks as if he's levitating.

As everything slows down, the last words of the

song whisper, *for he never rode that do-own bou-ound traaaaain.*

It winds to a stop and everyone looks around at each other as if they've been under a hypnosis spell.

In the weekdays, when the fair is quiet, Jono will go out into a nearby town or to one of the piers.

Me and Connie will follow him all day like spies, tracking him over railway bridges, hiding behind log flume engine rooms and ice cream vans.

He goes to a snooker hall called Harry's Hustle and I know he goes to that one mainly because Tammy works there.

One stormy day at the end of summer, we saw him stumbling home. It was around teatime and me and Connie had found a scrapyard to play in, full of old fairground props that were rusted and beaten from the weather.

We'd be leaving The Dips for another site in the next few days, so we were exploring one last time.

Jono was drunk. He was carrying his snooker queue. His hair was wet with rain and snot poured from each nostril.

We don't like seeing him like that and to this day we've sworn to keep it secret.

He was crying, bawling like a little baby. Before he got to our trailer he snapped his snooker queue over his knee. I knew it wasn't over any game he was weeping about.

It wasn't that at all.

SHE OWNS ACRES

She owns acres of land across the isle. She's the proprietor of the great green dips and the streets of terraced housing around the boardwalk. She owns the ghost pier in the south and the new pier in the north. She leases the docks to ship repairers, restaurateurs, psychics, cinema owners and slot machine arcades.

She owns the museums and medicine shows, the ballrooms and a haunted old hotel called The Finniland Inn. She's wealthy beyond imagination.

Let me tell you about her.

She lives alone on a stud farm, way out of town in the middle of the island, beyond the valley bluffs and The Dips and the rainwater reservoirs.

The farmhouse she lives in is a grand Georgian mansion with balconies and porches and four-poster beds. She's the only person who lives there, and it's a ruin.

She's a collector of things. Specific things. For example, there's a barn filled with prosthetic legs. Some of them are the really old kind, with the Victorian lock mechanism.

Another barn is full of used postcards and family photograph albums of people she's never met.

In the corner of that room is a fully rebuilt hippopotamus skeleton, three digital harpsichord pianos, a guillotine and a heap of broken fax machines.

The smallest barn, closest to the house and

padlocked with sixteen types of industrial lock, is a very sacred and holy place, and is always maintained in weatherproof paint and insulation.

Inside the barn is a shrine in memory of Corrine, her beloved and stillborn baby.

Every wall is papered with Polaroid prints and posters of mother and child.

Moroccan lights hang from the ceiling so that the patterned colours in the room are kaleidoscopic and dreamlike.

Candles are lit, incense burns, there are looped audio recordings of hospital rooms and midwives on maternity wards.

Corrine is illuminated, the small form of her in the centre, petrified in a biology jar. She is pale and translucent, suspended forever.

She doesn't go in there, except on the child's birthday. People are paid to maintain the barn, and read stories to the baby.

At night, the lights of the great house stay lit.

Sometimes you can hear her beyond the great swaying magnolia curtains of her high bedroom, saying over and over in prayer:

"I love you Corrine."

"I loved you Corrine."

"Sweet baby Corrine."

A bath will run, then another, and they are never attended to.

In summer the kids come down from the coastal terraces. They walk from either of the piers across fields of spiked gauze and thickets.

They'll approach in small groups, wielding sticks. They wear daisy necklaces, school ties tied around their heads, mud war paint smeared under their eyes like Rambo. There'll be sweat on their brows and cuts on their legs from the long journey.

Tonight the Moon is full and high. It hovers over the field like a magic saucer.

One kid leads the group. He is wearing a Native American headdress and holds a hubcap shield. He knows where he is going.

He walks the kids in a perfect single file, around a mirror pond and a privy of stacked hay bales.

In a clearing, an old ride-on lawnmower painted completely in fluorescent yellow glows like a star.

They line up at the window of Corrine's barn, the kid in the Comanche feathers stacking one, two, then three milk crates on top of each other, accepting a fifty pence piece from anyone brave enough to lay eyes on Corrine.

The lead kid carries out his rote tasks like someone who has done this many times.

Some of the children retreat at the last minute and run back to the group, shocked by their own imaginations.

Some stand there, transfixed by what's in front of them; locked in inquisitive suspense.

One kid throws up.

Another starts crying.

"I seen it I seen it," one's saying, her eyes wide as frisbees, running back to the group.

"What did you see?" another asks.

"I seen its big head and little dingaling and one hand pointing out at me, it was just staring and now I think I've got the curse..."

LUNA
THE FIRE EATER

"What's my name?" Luna's saying.

It's July on Coral Island, the peak of the season.

She's wandering up and down the promenade at two in the afternoon, lost in a dream of herself.

"I can't for the life of me remember what my name is."

Thinking about something from a long time ago, she laughs, shakes her head and says, "Anyway, I said I wouldn't do it for a penny less. What do they take me for up there, a mime artist?"

Somebody passes and shouts, "Luna, Luna, it's LUNA!" and points, but Luna doesn't notice.

She hobbles on, eyes fixed on the ground, muttering to herself, wrapped in layers of coats and winter scarves. She wears chunky black wraparound sunglasses that an Italian crime boss might have worn in the 1980s.

"Get yourself a new fire eater I told 'em. Go and get an amateur like Lenny Lava, see how that washes."

Things haven't been the same since they made her quit smoking. Breakfast isn't as satisfying. Drinking tea seems somehow incomplete. All the new smells are invasive, and she preferred it when she couldn't taste black pudding.

But it's the insomnia that's the real kick in the teeth. She hasn't slept properly since *Eldorado* was cancelled.

Luna loved her cigs.

Making a sharp right off the promenade road, she ducks into a junk shop called Work & Play.

She buys a deck of cards with naked ladies on the back. Two diamanté pint glasses celebrating the wedding of Prince Charles and Lady Diana. She buys a flick comb and an electric shock handshake prank.

Somehow, these are the only things that make any sense in the new world.

In a mini-mart called Declan's Trolley-Dolly she ghosts towards the freezer aisle.

She thinks Declan hasn't noticed, but Declan knows Luna.

Declan keeps his eyes trained on a small black and white monitor that sits behind the stickle-brick till.

Luna sets her walking stick down and heaves the freezer open. She pulls a huge lamb joint out, opens her jacket and slips it under her arm. On her way out, she says, "Maybe next time Deccy, see ya."

"Lunaaaaa..." Deccy says as she trails off.

On she goes, away from the promenade into the old town.

She stops at an electric cigarette shop called Ace of Vapes, and goes inside.

"Michael, Josh, Emily," Luna says, and everyone

replies with a "Hi Luna!".

They're stood behind a glass counter that divides the shop. They're dressed in identical blue polo shirts and baseball caps. The caps have a spade sewn into the peak.

Luna knows what she's looking for.

"Let me see. I'll take three Peach Passion. I'll have fifteen packets of the spearmint nicotine gum. Give me a couple of patches, WITHOUT the sticky outer bit," She struggles to open her handbag. "You know, they bring me out in a rash."

She brings out a vape with a carved ivory handle. The carved patterns are of dragons, huge eyeballs and flowering stars. It's like an instrument of death from old Siam.

She takes the lamb joint from her coat, sets it on the counter, and loads the vape with one of the liquid cartridges.

When she switches it on, it makes a Super Mario 'power up' noise.

For the next half hour, Luna puts on a show. She pulls hard on the filter and exhales intricate vapour smoke rings, snowflakes and spider's webs.

Then she really turns it on.

Orangutans swing from giant trees. Unicorns graze under a frozen waterfall. Soldiers jump from battlefield trenches and charge at each other with rifles.

From the street, a crowd has gathered. Someone whispers, "Sue, it's Luna, look! Pass me the baby."

People take photographs with their phones. They

shout for requests, and Luna obliges: "Do King Kong on the Empire State Building, catching the aeroplane!"

By the end, even Declan from Declan's Trolley-Dolly, flanked by two policemen, is applauding.

Luna walks home, oblivious, and says to herself:

"Don't think I won't go down to the South Pier. Don't think I won't go there. You want class, you pay for class. The fifties were over a decade ago. Get with the times!"

At night, she sits at the computer, editing grainy videos of Billy Fury together.

She sends them to the few friends she still has, old carnies who, like her, haven't yet passed over to the great palladium palace in the sky.

FIRST NIGHT
OF THE HOLIDAYS

This is the beginning. The slot-machine zoetrope of pier weekends, of caravan park palladiums, long fields of maize and rye that flicker and blink like eyelashes in the dusk, lines of hawser rope coiled around peeling bollards on the wharf. Fish guts rotten in the nose. The stink of life.

Night draws in as we near the gated field. Static caravans stretch out like sleeping dogs. Everything connected, everything new. I dozed on blanketed backseats down miles of Whitsun motorway to be here, to witness this mystery. I slip my shoes off and feel cool grass between my toes. In the near distance, a crowd has gathered at the banks of a canal. A man has waded in up to his waist. He's pushing something up from the water. Another man and a woman grab the thing from his hands and lay it down on the grass. The woman is distraught. She's frantic, pressing her mouth against it.

"My child," she's saying, "My baby..."

Something is moving toward where the lights are.

DOWNHOME SPECIAL

We call it The Bullet Train. Its real name is the Downhome Special, but when you ride its roof, you feel like a bullet.

It whizzes around Coral Island once in a blue moon.

No one can explain why.

It's not registered to any train network or freight company. It doesn't pull coal or deliver diggers to limestone quarries. It doesn't carry any passengers.

Some say it's a ghost train.

People spend their whole lives trying to spot it, and fail miserably.

Not us though.

Me and my friends, we not only saw it god knows how many times, we used to surf it.

Yessir, we did.

We'd catch it on its terrific and supernatural trajectory through the train yard, which was in a small town we lived in called Carham, not far from that infamous place known as the South Pier.

I swear that when it reached top speed I'd go into this altered state. It made life outside of the train feel pathetic and flimsy, a daft charade. Like my Earthly existence was a ride on the Tunnel of Love or one of those crappy North Pier attractions.

What I'm saying is that riding the bullet train made you feel invincible.

We used to sing a song:

Riding on the roof of the train
Iko-iko-an-ney
If the police come we'll only do it again
Jack-a-mo-fin-nan-ney

This is how we'd surf the Bullet Train:

We'd hang off a beam in this rickety tunnel that runs through a mountain.

On one side was a sheer cliff face that dropped down into the violent and angry sea they call Estrangia.

You'd know the Downhome Special was nearby, because you'd get this weird feeling in your bones and then suddenly the air would be full of golden motes that smelled like burning coal and steam. So we'd leg it, up to the tunnel that was held together by these old wooden joists that went up and straight, like a hot-cross bun.

My god, when it comes, you never forget it.

The first two times I was too afraid to drop but the third time Leo Gaskill stood on my fingers and I had no choice.

That rush, it's the truest feeling on God's Earth.

You get taken around the whole island. Your heart beats through your mouth, your nostrils sizzle, your eyes water and your hair is pinned back to your head.

You see everything: the container port and its mournful working cranes, stooping and lifting in the black. You see the dead on the water doing their funeral tango. You whoosh into the leafy centre of the island and see the gypsy fair at The Dips, straining to stay alight like a faulty candle, and further down, all the beautiful big wicker men cursing the horizon.

Much as I hate it up there, the North Pier is a sight to behold, a bright Catherine wheel of neon.

There'd be three or four of us at a time on the roof, and if we could catch our breath for a second, we'd glance at one another and burst into laughter.

The thing about my friends and I was that we were a fearless bunch that went by the name of The Grey Harpoons.

We weren't afraid of anything.

We looked death in the eye.

We laughed at the daft old bastard.

We made a fool of death.

We met when most of us were locked up in a borstal called St. Elmo's Catholic Correction School, like a prison for naughty kids. We hated it there but they taught us how to box, how to lay a brick and how to get up in the morning.

Leo Gaskill was our leader. He'd been there a year or two before most of us arrived. He'd been caught holding up a jewellery store with a gun. Only it wasn't a gun, it was one of those spud guns that shoot out bits of potato. He got four years for that.

Leo gave us our name, taught us how to act and look after each other. We became good friends.

As chance had it, we were released from St. Elmo's

27

on the same day.

The borstal was on the East of the island near a sprawl of static trailers known as Caravan City.

Gaskill suggested he and I walk there. He knew a man called Gold who could get us a couple of scrambler bikes so we could make it home.

When we got to Caravan City, we walked for miles through rows of motorhomes and trailers, portable loos and washhouses. There were big rattling generators that belched out diesel fumes, quad bike rentals, snooker rooms and rickety old bars that were built from corrugated metal.

We came up to Gold's Motorcycle repair shack.

He was stood outside in a blue jumpsuit. His face was covered in oil, but his hair was a bright golden mane that went down his back.

"Think you can ride it?" he asked me, after he'd given Gaskill his fastest scrambler.

This one, he said, was his favourite. It was sprayed all in black with gold shocks.

"I know I can," I said, and kick started it.

By this point, Gaskill was long gone, down a dirt track between the caravans.

"Well," Gold said. "You ride good, Jackie Boy, y'hear me?"

And I felt a huge pride that Gaskill had told him my name.

I saw a lot of Gaskill that summer. I learned to surf the Bullet Train. I grew up. I started to box for the South Pier Boy's Club and by Christmas, all my time was spent in O'Hearne's gym just off the crumbling parade road.

The Grey Harpoons drifted apart. But we all knew that gangs were for the summer, the wild rush of summer, and that winter was for solitude.

By the end of next spring, I was kicking around the South Pier again. I met up with most of the old gang, but I couldn't find Leo Gaskill anywhere.

He wasn't in any of the arcades or snooker halls.

I asked in the bowling alley and Tasha said she hadn't seen him strike since last year.

All around the North Pier I asked, but I didn't expect him to be there anyway because he thought it was full of snobs.

One day I was walking across the sand dunes that surround the great green expanse they call The Dips.

He was coming up from Carham way, where I was headed. He was pushing the scrambler bike that Gold had given him to ride home on last year.

"Leo!" I shouted.

Leo smiled.

"Where've you been?" I asked him.

Leo smiled again.

"Well?"

He brought me in close.

"Remember those lizards we found at the back of Maccomb's Pet Shop last year?"

"Yeah?"

"Well, they weren't lizards at all. I knew it at the time. They were young alligators. I recognised them from that movie *Alligator,* where the American kids have them as pets and end up flushing them down the toilet when they get too big. They grow into adults down there and start eating people."

"What did you do with them?"

"Come with me," Gaskill said.

We went to this big pond that was near the railway tunnel, above the sea of Estrangia. Gaskill looked happy, more grounded than I'd ever seen him. He'd put on weight and his raw energy was somewhere else now, outside of him somehow.

"Watch," he said, and picked up a huge stick.

He walked over to the pond and began stabbing the tip of stick into the bed.

One, two, three.

Four, five, six.

Gaskill looked back at me:

"They'll come on twelve. They always do."

Seven, eight, nine.

Ten, eleven...

On cue, four full-sized alligators rose out of the water like monsters from Atlantis.

I reeled back onto the wet grass.

They were enormous. Gaskill was calm, using the stick to introduce me.

"This one's called Tommy. That big fella at the back, his name's Spike. This girl here is Winnie and the one with three legs is Wayne."

"Wayne?" I laughed.

"Yeah, Wayne," Gaskill said.

He crouched down at the water's edge and put the

big stick between Wayne's jaws.

Everything was calm.

I thought it was weird though, because I smelled something I recognised. The smell of a furnace, of steam, of electricity fizzing down a rail.

When the air began to fill with dancing cinders, I knew what was happening.

It was coming from the railway above us.

I tried to shout to Leo but the great sound came quick and drowned me out.

The Bullet Train whizzed past, travelling with a greater speed and ferocity as I'd ever seen it. The front of the train - an iron cowcatcher - was half ignited with the faint blue ghost of a flame.

Leo was caught up with the gators. He didn't notice until the last minute. He stood up when the train appeared, caught in terrific shock, petrified.

I saw it in his face, the look of death. He went off balance and fell in the pond.

I didn't see him then because there was too much water splashing about. I think it was the alligator called Spike who got hold of him. It rolled him three or four times until the thrashing stopped and they both went under.

That was the end of Leo Gaskill.

SO THAT I DREAM NO MORE

Robert had been playing with the dog all morning, trying to teach it the 'which hand' trick, but Prinnie had ignored his instructions and instead pawed at his frail fists until he gave in.

It seemed that he couldn't even earn a dog's respect.

Then there was Leanne, who had grown tired of Robert's backbone, or lack of one, and Robert knew this, accepted it and ambled on doggedly, in his own way.

Clearly, there was still a relationship there in some form, an unspoken comportment that what they had was preferable to the rigmarole of being alone in the great world.

But the dog, the dog was stupid, Robert thought. And besides, he didn't have his right voice today.

After that episode, he'd begun imagining The Ghost Train, and had to go back to bed. If he began imagining The Ghost Train on any day, he'd have to lie in a darkened room for an hour to clear his thoughts, or he'd be no use to anyone.

He closed his eyes and the morning began to drift. Eventually, the image of The Ghost Train dissipated.

Noon.

Leanne came home with a jangle and a thud.

As usual, a force field of perfume surrounded her. The hairdressers on the North Parade would ply her with it until she was drunk on her own laughter, and pay for any old do.

The smell woke Robert from his meditation.

He heard a bag drop to the floor and a flint being sparked. Then the light appeared.

Leanne was at the bedroom door. A Chinese dragon of smoke chandelled up from her fingers and surrounded her head. Her familiar silhouette, tall and imposing, curved like an upright manatee.

Robert grimaced internally.

"Let's do it again."

"We've done it already this morning!" Robert protested, undoing his belt.

"It's the only way it'll happen," said Leanne, dropping the cigarette onto the laminate. She ground it with her stiletto heel as she came toward him.

Leanne got on top and things returned to darkness.

In his mind, Robert saw a wooden pay booth. There was a fruit machine next to it spewing out blue tickets, like it was stuck on jackpot.

To his left, there was a huge oak door with fangs at the top and bottom, like some demon's mouth.

He was in a queue, and the queue began to move, carrying him along like he was caught in a riptide, toward the mouth. He could hear the click-clack of wheels on a track.

Fear, ice-cold fear, shot through him. His heart fluttered like a moth's wing.

Then suddenly he moaned.

Leanne stopped, and the light returned.

Robert gasped.

For a minute there, he was almost back on The Ghost Train.

From the hallway, Leanne was talking:

"...which means we'll have to walk. The Pier's heaving and the alleyways are just as bad. I forgot: it's bank holiday. Tourist nightmare."

Robert swung his legs over the side of the bed and pulled his trousers up.

"I prefer the walk anyway," he mumbled.

"What's wrong, why are you talking like that?"

"I haven't got my right voice today," Robert said, fixing his glasses.

"Today of all days," said Leanne to the mirror, pampering at the back of her hair bouquet.

They moved through swarms of Whitsun holiday goers, shuffling through the mob on the North Parade at first, then off the promenade to The Alleys, the labyrinthine network of back roads and stoops and crooked balconies that washing hung from and satellite dishes tried desperately to escape, stretching themselves unnaturally toward open sky like rusty sunflowers.

Robert preferred it here, in the shade.

They continued on, down ginnels of tearooms and old bed and breakfasts.

It was hot, sticky hot, and Robert's white shirt became translucent against his skin. He loosened his tie.

The old pubs began to appear.

Outside The Bull Inn, a man was selling puppies from a cardboard box.

Another man in a camel overcoat handed over fifty notes for a merle basset pup, with a frozen leg of lamb thrown in as a dowry.

He put the pup under his arm and buttoned up his Crombie.

The poor thing's going to suffocate, Robert thought, turning his neck as he walked.

Leanne didn't notice. She smoked long Rothmans and wobbled down the road, talking to a friend on the phone. Every now and then a stiletto heel would scrape a cobble. She put her friend on loudspeaker so that everybody could hear.

Leanne said:

"I know luvvie... I know. We'll get there. We have to make them *want* to fertilise."

Leanne's friend was coaching her through a situation.

At a pub called The Moon Underwater, they stopped.

Leanne marched in and ordered herself a gin and tonic, and half a Landlord for Robert, who sat down at a table under a great mirror.

Robert thought his moustache looked wrong in the mirror, and tried to fix it by moving his hat into different positions.

He also noticed that the beer mats on the table were a kind of tarot.

One said QUEEN OF PENTACLES. There was a picture of a glass of cider with a half Moon and dagger inside.

One said THE LOVERS with a picture of a bottle of Champagne and a capuchin monkey balanced on top. The monkey was covering its eyes.

One said DEATH and had a picture of a ghost train coming out of a great tunnel, with fangs at the top and bottom, like some demon's mouth.

Robert hurried to the bar, downed Leanne's gin and tonic, then immediately ordered another. The second was a double.

Leanne interrupted her phone call, put her hand over the receiver and mouthed, *what's got into you.*

Robert secretly laughed to himself. He felt giddy.

Ghost Train, he thought.

Outside, Leanne was going on: "...and god knows, I don't want you to be there. Wait for me opposite, in one of the noodle bars. And for crying out loud, watch your drink intake! Migraines, Robert, migraines. First your voice, now raging alcoholism! What next..."

They had come into the Old Chinatown area of the North Parade.

The air had cooled by now, the afternoon dulled to a mournful hum, an agreed truce in lieu of the coming night.

The streets narrowed again here. The flats, painted

proudly in red and green, were miniature, stacked on top of each other like sardine tins, a single port-hole for light.

Every so often, in the middle of a cluster of tene-ments, there would be an imitation Buddhist temple built in stucco, surrounded by iron fences and over-flowing industrial bins.

Robert loved their secrecy, their thrilling privacy. It was as far away from a ghost train as you could be.

Further on, he became transfixed by bright, flash-ing peep show windows and unmarked bookmakers. Leanne clucked her tongue every time they passed one.

Eventually, at a Cantonese chip shop called The Kowloon, they stopped.

Leanne composed herself, fixed Robert's tie, and stepped in.

There was a counter, chip fryers and cooling trays that gargantuan spring rolls and battered mackerel sat behind.

Robert could smell the wonderful aroma of plum sauce, Szechuan spices and satay. Whole ducks hung from meat hooks.

Leanne turned to the window, a handkerchief over her mouth. She looked at Robert and whis-pered, "You do it."

Behind the counter stood a little boy with a bowl cut and his front teeth missing. Robert pulled his lips apart and stuck out his tongue.

The boy pivoted on a flip-flop and smiled.

"Take your order?" a man in an apron said,

drying his hands.

"I'm sorry. We're here for Bixia," Robert whispered.

The boy ran away.

The man escorted them through the kitchen and to a space in the back where people sat in annexed computer booths.

Leanne was bothered. She dabbed sweat from her face with a handkerchief. Her new hair had gone flat.

The room was thick with smoke. It was clearly being used as a sort of Internet café. The computers were bulky old Amstrads and Acers, and Robert wondered how computers that old could even connect to the Internet.

Some of the people were on betting sites. Some were watching videos of Asian pop bands, twelve people on a stage doing intricate and synchronised dancing.

They went beyond there, stepping over a huge mop and bucket into a brightly lit hallway where framed photographs of very important Chinese politicians hung from the walls. They stared down at Robert like they knew about The Ghost Train.

By now, the effects of the drink were wearing thin and he could feel it nearing.

The man left them at a carpeted stairwell.

It was full of couples standing in a line that reached from the bottom to the very top.

One woman was in a wheelchair. Her partner had to hoist her up every step, and hold the chair until the queue moved.

Another couple wore matching sheepskin overcoats. A woman held a baby doll in her arms, and rocked it as if it was real.

The people in the queue were mostly impatient and tetchy.

They parted for a woman who walked down the stairs very slowly. She wore nothing but a dressing gown. Her hair was wet.

She looked a pale grey colour, like something had been given to, or taken from her.

On the wall next to Leanne, a sign read:

BIXIA YUANJIN
FERTILITY PRIESTESS

Robert remembered something.

A long time ago, there had been a picture postcard.

The picture postcard was of a deckchair attendant talking to a woman.

She was sat on a beach, drinking a flute of Champagne. She wore a bathing suit.

The attendant was leaning toward her. A speech bubble said, "You must come again, it really is an attractive front."

Somehow, he remembers it this way, like a cheap innuendo, but somehow sacred, too.

Robert had placed a fortune teller miracle fish into her palm that day, and told her that a good omen was about to occur, or had already arrived.

Leanne had laughed her drunk laugh. She had been stood up by her date, so Robert was her knight in shining armour, her saviour.

Yes, that's how he liked to remember it.

At the top of the stairs, the door opened.

Leanne suddenly pressed very tightly against Robert and squeezed his hand.

The girl that opened the door wore the same striped apron as the man in the chip shop; only hers was pink and white, striped on the vertical.

It was Annabelle Twice, the girl from their road. She must have only left school this year.

Leanne blushed.

Annabelle Twice smiled gently and said, "Please." She took Leanne's hand.

Leanne looked back with tears in her eyes.

It was strange seeing her like this, so vulnerable.

Through a crack in the door, Robert saw an old tin bathtub full of a white, watery liquid, like milk of magnesia.

A woman with a high ponytail was stood next to a room divider that a great dragon stared back from.

The woman wore a velvet red dress with high shoulders. She was brushing her long black hair in a mirror.

Robert saw Annabelle Twice removing Leanne's clothing. Leanne was scared rigid. Her eyes had gone to the back of her head. They looked glossy and buffed, like dud pearls. Her poor body was pale and bloodless, cleanly shaven all over.

He realised he hadn't seen her naked in years. Then he felt a terrible love for her, a terrible feeling of love and guilt and sadness that washed over him like a plague.

In the street, he had already started imagining The Ghost Train.

It came charging through his stomach and into his head at full speed.

There were shining new safety bars and fenders and screaming skulls at the front. The registration plate read LAND OF THE LOST. It had been preparing for him.

He hurried back to The Moon Underwater. He tried the gin trick again, but two, then three doubles made no difference.

The Ghost Train was angry.

He stopped imagining and started remembering.

It was somebody's birthday: identical twins, children whom he attended nursery with. They were in front of him, holding balloons. The balloons said FIVE.

His mother was there, a blurred face among other adults, but she was far away and he couldn't hear.

Robert looked in the pub mirror and realised he had been guided by the force of fear for all of his life, and this was its genesis.

The memory consumed him.

In the memory, he was strapped into The Ghost Train by a man with silver teeth.

As soon as it jolted forward, he screamed.

The Ghost Train hadn't even made it into the

tunnel.

Robert had gone into a kind of epileptic trance. A voice came out of him that wasn't his, low and guttural, thick with catarrh. He said ancient things, a made up language of the old gods and devils.

He was frothing at the mouth, choking.

They had to stop the train and get him off. Someone recorded it with a video camera, the whole thing, and it was shown later on a reality television show that used canned laughter.

Robert understood that above terror, the unflinching arrow of embarrassment was the one that cut through his armour cleanest.

And stumbling from The Moon Underwater through the back streets of Coral Island North Pier, he guided himself unconsciously.

There were points when he felt as if he was floating, being pulled by a cold magnetism.

In the side alley, it was there, it was all there, just as he remembered; the brown pay booth, the fruit machine that was stuck on jackpot.

He saw the door with the fangs, like some demon's mouth.

It spoke to him, and he listened like someone who has been searching for years, blind in a forest, a dead forest where terrible dreams go to die, and suddenly there is a break in the dense eternity, and a light.

He heard the squeal of brakes behind the demon's mouth, and something slowing to a stop.

He moved toward it, to his inevitable.

THE WEREWOLF

The Werewolf got made redundant today.

Danny Gloom mentioned it on his way down from The Gasworks, the walk-through ghost house he works at. Our friend Redmo confirmed it over a beer in The Calico Girl later that afternoon.

Both of them said that The Werewolf hadn't taken it too well.

He was always one for the amateur dramatics, I thought, but this might just push him over the edge.

We were all worried.

I saw him later in a comedy club called Quids Inn, sat at a table on his own.

He was still wearing the full body suit, which was made of heavy cotton and black imitation fur. The mask with the red eyes and flashing white fangs was on a seat next to him.

Even that looked sad.

He sat hunched over a double whisky, stirring it slowly. I swear I saw a tear or two fall into the glass.

I thought about going over, but then something happened.

There was a comedian on stage, but The Werewolf wasn't really listening to him.

"What's your story, Skip?" the comedian asked.

The Werewolf ignored it.

"Hey, White Fang. What's the trouble? Full Moon tonight? Seriously though…"

You could see what he was trying to do.

The Werewolf put one hand up, as if to say *leave me alone*, before knocking his whiskey back neat. I should have stepped in then.

"Hey Teen Wolf! Didn't you see the sign on the door? No pets allowed."

Somebody in the audience giggled.

Another person laughed.

The Werewolf looked over his shoulder. The comedian said:

"Now I've got your attention. What's the matter son, caught a furball?"

Then everybody laughed.

But The Werewolf stood up, and the room fell silent, like a huge black curtain had fallen down.

The comedian, who already looked stupid in an oversized yellow suit and red polka dot tie, looked even more stupid now, because the arse dropped out of him.

See, The Werewolf was pretty big.

What happened next shocked everybody.

He started howling.

He howled the first time and there was no reaction. But he turned to the audience as if to say *play along*.

He did it again and there was a giggle from the back of the room, the same person who'd giggled earlier.

Awwwwwwwoooooooo.

The next minute The Werewolf was on the table. He'd put his mask back on.

46

Whoever was operating the spotlight took it away from the comedian and projected it high up against a black curtain, so it looked like The Werewolf was howling to a full Moon.

The crowd went ballistic. They cheered and gathered around him and bought him drinks all night until he could no longer stand.

He was a great Werewolf, everyone on the island agreed.

That night he slept in his car. There were photographs on the dashboard of a man with a pair of golden doubloons over his eyes. There were other pictures too. One of a family.

He dreamed of icebergs. Vast, frozen plains that stretched out forever. He saw himself as a wolf, travelling across the Arctic.

In the dream, there was half a caribou carcass in his mouth. He was covered in blood and he was happy.

The next morning, Danny Gloom and I brought coffee and doughnuts to the car, expecting him to be awake, groggy but rejuvenated.

Only the car was empty, and The Werewolf was gone.

We never saw him again.

I heard he'd disappeared into the Forest of Dreams, on the South East of the Island, where real wolves run in packs, and tall mysterious wicker men guard the coastline like skeleton trees.

THE WEREWOLF

CORAL ISLAND PICTUREHOUSE

There's something magical about sitting in a dark cinema, staring up at a projector screen with perfect strangers either side of you, like it's some communal living room in outer space. It's a weekday ritual for us. We're drawn together like moths to a flame. Let me tell you.

There's an agreed silence when the lights go down. Everybody tunes into the hush and whisper, the rustle of jackets going under seats, the drowsy aroma of warm popcorn seeping through the exits like teargas, only the kiss is non-toxic. It's delivered by some siren up there from a Hollywood studio and lands right on the inner-antenna. The one you never knew you had.

There's something about it that says, this isn't just some pay-per-view money machine, some pier-side peepshow. This is something else, something higher. An incantation. We're lifted in some way, changed by a shared vision: *Lost Highway. The Big Sleep. Terminator 2. Nightmare Alley. Nightcrawler. The Blue Dahlia. Blade Runner. The Goonies.*

Outside, the rain plays a humdrum-rhumba against

the promenade windowpane. Blue-green, sea-green, green-grey. An afternoon funeral tango. The world expands and recedes with the rolling tide. Each day plays out like a series of films, a re-run of the last, a low budget sequel.

It's half past four on a Wednesday afternoon. The credits roll. We stay seated. Me, Adam Battle and the Di Santo twins. Harry the Crab, Jody King and the newlyweds (Richard and Trish). Lozzer, Tom Crock and Omar. Nikki Ormesher and her dad.

The lights go up, and we return to ourselves.

AFTER THE CLOSURE OF CORAL ISLAND PICTUREHOUSE

Picturehouse, we loved you. Where did you go in the shimmer of our black shoreline, our proud black shoreline. Where did you go? Disappeared with the trawlerboats and markets. And your midnight showings will be forever in our memory. We hid under your starless canopy. We travelled through time. We gave our souls as admission fee. And when Dempsey died in the exit aisle. Stabbed with a rusted thing. Bled from the inside and out. You soaked up his blood on your patterned floor while you showed us adverts for improved chewing gum. Do you remember? I stand on the vacant plot now, the flattened land. Iron frames jut out of the concrete. The old smell and the view of the sea. The feeling of space, of hollow space. Picturehouse, they burned you down. They burned you down and we left you to rot.

LETTER TO SHANNON

I saw you on my way home from the North Pier Palace Palladium.

I used to park the cars there, see, for the rich people, the ballroom dancing types. They'd turn up in expensive vehicles, wearing tuxedos and evening dresses. Sometimes they'd throw their car keys up in the air and expect me to catch them. They wouldn't even stop to say thanks.

I worked there from when I was twelve. I grew up in a Wimpy drive-thru, so all the dragster kids would let me roll the cars in when they were too drunk to navigate the tight bend. That was when I was five or six. I grew up pretty fast.

But that's not why I'm writing. You know all of this.

Did you forget about our night? I didn't.

Let me remind you.

It was the end of summer, or what they call an Indian summer, and most of the holiday crowds had packed up and left.

There was that sadness everywhere, that chip-paper-in-the-wind feeling, like it was the last scene of a movie and there'd be no sequel.

You feel it most if you live here.

You think it'll be great when the tourists leave and you can breathe again, but it's not like that at all. The familiar ghosts reappear, the sun starts crying and all the pier illuminations go woozy and weak, like they're drunk. Instantly, you regret the exodus.

Anyway, that evening the light was beautiful, the crepuscular light that the distant refinery sky gifted us.

We hadn't met at this point, but I was guided to you by a feral and fearless seagull that snaffled my phone out of my hand as I was dangling my legs off the boardwalk.

I was picking at a cone of chips that rested between my thighs. In that moment I was pretty happy.

I was playing a game on my phone called *Snake*, only half the screen was bust and my lives would last fifteen seconds at most.

The feeling of dying and being reborn over and over had me hooked.

I guess the seagull got mixed up and thought the old phone was one of my chips. It calmly walked with it around the marine diner into a forecourt where the Picturehouse used to be.

There you were, on a bench in jeans and work boots, a beret on your head.

You were covered in paint.

You'd been working on an ocean scene in one of the Pier gift shops, you told me later, a giant octopus guarding a treasure chest. It didn't pay much but you were bored, you said. It was the fourth week of a holiday with your parents and things had slowed to a laborious slog.

Yeah, you were an artist. That's how I still see you.

I hope you didn't give that up.

So, you picked my phone out of the seagull's beak as if it was the most natural thing in the world. You were holding it up as I approached, like it was a gun you'd found in the gutter. You were laughing, out of shock I think, and your hand was over your mouth. But I could tell you were laughing by the beautiful shape your eyes made.

And that's where we told each other our own stories, our pasts and futures, right there on the bench.

We must have talked for two, maybe three hours.

In front of us, there was a big clock hanging from the front of an abandoned pub. The sign said GUINNESS TIME, and the clock hadn't moved for years. That's how it felt for me, like time was frozen.

Was it the same for you?

After, I told you I thought I was in love, and you laughed, so I pretended to cry, and you laughed some more, and you came right out with it.

"So show me a good time," you said, twisting your hoop earring, playing along with the script.

Of course I did.

I'd stolen one of the rich folks' wallets, see. I did that a lot, as a kind of revenge for the way they treated me.

I opened the wallet and took out the owner's driver's licence. He looked like a professional, a man of authority I thought, like a politician or a brain surgeon.

I didn't feel an ounce of guilt.

Also, you pointed out that I looked nothing like him.

"It's okay, they never check," I said. "Besides, Lavelle will be on the gate, and me and Big Lavelle go back a long way."

The man in the wallet was also the owner of a North Pier Palladium membership card.

These cards were rare, and allowed entry into the Diorama section of the North Pier. That's where the real high rollers go.

This was the part you loved the most: everything in there is free.

Inside the Diorama, we wondered around wide-eyed.

There's this huge water tank where beautiful men and women wearing mermaid tails do a kind of underwater ballet, weaving in and out of kingdoms that look like Atlantis.

There are illusionists and mind readers and whirling dervish dancers, masseuses and mime artists and imitation opium dens with the cots and long pipes.

You can eat anything you want.

We picked at huge shrimp from beds of ice, ate suckling pig that span on spits. We smoked shisha in elegant Bedouin tents.

It was like we were in a movie, you with the beret over one eye like the old Hollywood actresses and the perfume I can still smell.

Jesus, I felt like a fuckin' king!

We went into the wondrous mirror maze and laughed at our elongated bodies. I piggybacked you all the way out onto the North Parade road. We stopped at a shelter and shared a blueberry slushie.

Out of nowhere, you said:

"Remember when forever meant forever?"

"What do you mean?"

"Time. It's moving so fast now. When I was a kid, summer was never-ending."

"This might seem a bit sudden but..."

I brought a half eaten bag of Haribo out of my pocket and we married each other with jelly rings, on Coral Island promenade.

You called me your *lover undiscovered*, after a song you'd been listening to.

You put one of your headphones in my ear, one in yours and we listened to it.

All night I sang it back to you and got the words wrong on purpose, and you pretended to get annoyed.

After the ceremony you said, "Come on, it's our honeymoon. Aren't you gonna get me drunk?"

We rode the cable car loop three times around and finished a bottle of White Lightning.

You told me about Rainland, how dull it is over there, and how you could see yourself living here one day. I said, "Me casa, su casa," but the joke didn't land.

From the cable car terminal, we walked down to the bluffs and bought paper LSD trips from a kid I knew called Hadlin.

Hadlin wore a scuffed old leather jacket and

squinted his eyes when he saw me.

"What you up to, Joe Nearly?" Hadlin smiled.

I smiled back at him. You said, "What's funny?"

"This is Shannon," I said. "She's from Rainland."

Hadlin said to you, "Aren't you meant to be back on the rock by now? It's the middle of September."

You said, "My dad booked us here 'til autumn. God knows why."

"Stay as long as you want," Hadlin said. He spat a chewy out and volleyed it into the boot of a passing car.

It took a long time to come up.

We were away from the pier then, walking along the sea wall towards Bungalow Bay, the cable cars passing over us like bloated seabirds.

That's how you described them. I remember: *bloated seabirds*.

Slowly, we began to see faces in trees, cloud people looking down at us laughing, and us laughing back.

At the peak of the trip we were drawn to this kid in the sand dunes. He wore powerful bifocals and a dressing gown. He was down on all fours, growling at us like a lion.

Did we actually see him or was that the LSD?

What do you think?

You took it all in your stride though, and didn't get spooked. It was me who eventually went quiet.

We'd been walking for three or four hours, see, and I knew our time was coming to an end.

It was getting light.

We stopped in the beach nature reserve and just

lay there in the reeds for an hour, hand in hand, watching the sky change.

We promised we'd follow each other on Instagram and I nodded as if had a computer or a phone good enough to be a part of that world.

Months later I realised that this couldn't have been possible anyway, because we hadn't even told each other our names.

As I watched you ghost over the dunes toward your caravan, I felt a lump in my throat, which sent a pang of anger shooting through the pharmaceutical curtain.

I knew it would be the last time I'd ever see you.

Do you remember now?

For a while I stood there on the slip road, waiting for something to happen, but you just kept getting smaller.

I watched you disappear.

Then the sea began to swell, hissing like it was angry, like it didn't have to pretend to be nice any more. I spat into it.

A ship appeared in the distance, carrying cranes and diggers and dismantling equipment toward the pier, which was sleeping peacefully.

I wanted to shout to it, to warn of what was about to happen.

I wanted to tell it that summer was over, and this was it, the end.

Autumn had come.

Shannon   *Oh Shannon*

remember summer

            that rainy summer

        before you went back to your

                 one-eyed

        city

HOLY JOE

On a deserted tip of the island, there's this tower.

At the top of the tower is a big silver ball.

At the top of the silver ball are six radio antenna that are shaped like lightning bolts.

I made them myself, out of plasterer's whisks, and stuck them up there in a force-ten gale. Then I sprayed them, and the whole tower the colour of mercury.

The tower was built in the fifties as a grain store, before being used as a moor for a Michelin blimp. After the blimp detached from its hook and floated away across Coral Bay, it was abandoned. So I claimed it.

I carried receivers and microphones up the ladder myself, and rigged it up to the mains of a roller rink next door.

Inside, I decorated it with pictures of Gene Vincent and Albert Finney, Lauren Bacall, Shelagh Delaney and Shakin' Stevens.

Soon after, I started the show.

I thought of the name when I was a kid. I just knew I was going to call it The Dancing Menagerie of Holy Joe and his Rock n' Roll Medicine Show.

I built it up from nothing.

These days, I broadcast to the whole island. The show beams into every arcade, ghost house, all-night tea room, rollercoaster ride, oddity museum, tramway, fish market, bingo hall, back alley brass house, car boot sale, mystery maze, bowling alley, old folks home, hermitage, snooker hall and soup kitchen on the island.

I'm everywhere.

You can't just play anything. You have to feel it out.

I'll start every show with *Break on Through* by The Doors.

After that, anything by:

Buddy Holly, Wanda Jackson or Eddie Cochran.

Shadow Morton and The Shangri-Las.

Van Morrison and Them.

Del Shannon.

The Spanish strut of Mink DeVille.

The Coral (It's in my contract).

I'll play possessed souls like Screamin' Jay Hawkins, Billie Holiday and the delicate, drifting angel, Skip James.

Between songs I might play snippets of The Shipping Forecast, Dylan Thomas poems, interviews with James Dean, or Richard Burton reading his diaries.

Radio highlights of boxing bouts from the forties.

Episodes of the detective show *Dragnet*.

An album I really love is Lou Reed's *Coney Island Baby*.

But we all know that Joe Meek is the undisputed KING of the airwaves!

Camille is my friend.

She comes to see me before the show starts. She

brings food, drink and bars of rock.

We sit there, sipping on a mix of Buckfast and White Lightning, that I call Tartan Turpentine. By midnight, I'm good and juiced, which is when I begin. I'll start by playing some background sounds and go over my intro:

Now let's hear some haunted, haunted rock n' roll!
Now do the dog!
Now do the Sphinx!
Do the ghost train!
Now curl up like a corpse!
Now do the exorcist!
Now do the resurrection!

All night, people text in, requesting songs. It's pointless because everything they ask for I've already lined up. The people of Coral Island and me, we're in sync.

While I'm on air, Camille runs an online tarot service. She's a mastermind at making money. She set up an automated thing where she'll give psychic readings without having to lift a finger. The cards flip at random and the computer generates some mumbo-jumbo that make the customers think they'll win the lottery one day, or discover the cure for a tropical disease, or die suddenly in a lead mine.

She charges fifteen quid a reading.

At this rate, she'll be a millionaire.

In the early hours, things start to unravel. People have told me this is their favourite part of the show.

I'm not proud of it, but I'll let some of my theories fly.

I'll tell them about the ley lines that run underneath the island. How they affect the fertility of women depending on where they live on either side of the magnetic field.

I'll tell them how music is a form of witchcraft.

I'll give the names of over-the-counter pills that stunt your growth or shrink your brain or turn testosterone into silly putty. I'll name some naturally growing plants and herbs that do the opposite.

I'll talk about the third eye, the human psychic eye, and how the elite governments want to suppress it by putting fluoride in our water.

I'll give co-ordinates for vast underground LSD bunkers that burrow under the hinterlands of Bungalow Bay.

When I've said my piece, I'll go back to the music. It'll be getting light by then, so I'll play some old movie scores for the tired taxi drivers and table dancers who are finishing up for the night. It helps them unwind.

I see all this as a kind of divine mission. It's my job, my place in the world. I connect the moods and minds of people all across the island: I soundtrack their lives.

POEM ON THE ALLEYWAY FLOOR

In the summer, they spray pig's blood over the farmer's fields around The Dips.

It's meant to keep the crows from eating the wheat and barley and the husks of corn that are sold to market down in Bungalow Bay.

But the smell.

The smell of rotten blood on the wind: it drives the tourists from Rainland crazy.

Me and Connie, we're used to it.

See, Jono sets the fair up at The Dips so often that the smell almost reminds us of home.

We like it here on Coral Island. We want to stay. The long drowsy days of wandering from the fair and ending up in Caravan City or the South Pier or Finniland, they are our golden hours.

We get up to allsorts:

We build dens.

We find wedding rings in rock pools.

We look at baby Corrine in the magic jar.

We look for clues to the pony ride flea market murders.

We pick out suspects in the promenade crowds.

We put laxatives in Space Raiders and feed them to seagulls, so they blitzkrieg the promenade crowds with bombs of pure white shit.

We talk about Mum.

We lie on our backs and pick out mum's face in cloud patterns, the prettiest patterns that are winged and angelic and radiate gold even when they have passed the sun.

One day we were ambling down from the chemical works near Finniland.

We'd spent the day exploring these huge rainwater reservoirs that stretch out beyond the cooling station towers.

We were near the small town of Carham.

Connie was sidewinding through an alleyway, trying to catch something under his foot. Every time he got close to it, a gust of wind would come and blow it a few yards in front of him. It was like it didn't want to be caught.

I ran in front of Connie so we had it surrounded.

It was a piece of paper with a poem written on. We didn't know who wrote it, or who it was written for. What we knew was that it was a kind of letter, or confession, something that the author wanted to say, but couldn't find a sound that was right for the feeling.

The only way they could express it was to picture the words in their mind's eye, then copy them onto paper.

Connie and me used to read it to each other.

We are attracted to the life-or-death, see, the real howls of pain and joy. We'd recite it at night, in the back of the trailer. We know it by heart.

The rest of summer was spent trying to track this person down using our detective instinct, but we didn't get a lead.

Here, I'll read it to you.

I saw a fleeting form
between the trees
the window cries
it crackles like a
Jones Brothers record
the firmament rages
to infinite symphonies
of impossibility
I close my eyes
I'm floating on a raft
I'm Tom Sawyer
I'm Huck Finn
I'm nothing at all

if that's how it feels
I can live with that -
Auntie Mo sits on the patio
a china cup
clasped between two wrinkled fingers
she knew about the car crash
outside of the bakery
before it even happened
if I could go back
I wouldn't change a thing
but I wish Shirley was still here
she wouldn't have let the family
fall apart
everyone fucks up
I won't let anyone tell me
we weren't happy
everyone can be happy in their imagination.

THE
GREAT LAFAYETTE

He's a shadow of the man he was. Pains me to say, but it's true. All of us think so. At one time he was champion of the island, a real hero. But all that has gone.

Gone.

Gone.

Gone.

The first thing you notice is he's lost weight. He's still gargantuan, don't get me wrong. But he's human now, the same as us. Fifteen years ago, I swear he was a giant, straight from *Jack And The Beanstalk*. You could put him in the Pier Palace and he'd fill the ballroom no problem. He had to travel in his own bus. He could wrestle bears, sometimes two at a time, and he could stop the wind with his laughter.

These days he's down to twenty stone. His clothes are too big and he looks hungry all the time.

Loose skin hangs from arms covered in faded seafaring tattoos: the scales of liberty, a topless geisha, a white-winged dove.

It's simple really: The Great Lafayette is struggling to come to terms with having been forced into retirement. To his credit, he hung on until the bitter end.

But the end wasn't pretty.

At the tail end of the nineties, another strongman, Mike Titanic, challenged Lafayette to a High Striker contest.

The High Striker is the hammer machine at the fairground. You'll find one on every corner on Coral Island North Pier.

See, Lafayette was one of the North Pier's main attractions. That's a pretty big deal. We're talking tens of thousands.

Mike Titanic was a lot younger than Lafayette, and a big man himself, nearly as big as The Big L.

Mike wanted L's place as the main man of the Pier. He knew that if he could win the High Striker contest, it would generate enough press to earn him top spot.

Naturally, Lafayette accepted.

On the day, lots of people showed up. There were reporters and TV cameras from local news stations.

To cut a long story short, Mike Titanic achieved the highest ever score on a 25-foot High Striker.

Lafayette who went second, *blew the bell off the top.* The striker went through the top of the machine and continued going up, until nobody could see it. Everybody cheered. Lafayette had won.

Only he hadn't.

Nobody told him there'd be a drug test.

What they found in his bloodstream could have powered the island for a month: petrol, barbiturates, amphetamines, uranium. But none of this was new to L. He was old school. He'd been running on uppers for decades.

Anyway, because of the scandal in the press, he was sacked. Titanic took his place.

These days, The Great Lafayette sits in his caravan all night, squeezing a Thighmaster between his thumb and forefinger, watching stock car racing on the TV.

He'll buy speed off the gang from Carham, the Grey Harpoons, who'll whizz over on scrambler bikes, kicking up dirt and dust with their tyre treads.

He'll surf Internet camera rooms, chatting to girls he calls his cherry bombs. They'll think nothing of taking four, five hundred quid off him in a couple of sessions.

Sometimes, in the early hours, we pass by his trailer. You can see him through a side window, stood at the kitchen counter. He'll be eating huge steaks with his bare hands, tormenting the dogs.

THE GREAT LAFAYETTE

FOURTH NIGHT
OF THE HOLIDAYS

Such nights were written by lunatic poets in bridewell drunk tanks. By madmen hanging off a midnight railway bridge. By pub singers drowning in rainwater reservoirs. Such nights were written for my brothers and me.

Caravan City, Coral Island:

Our mum and dad are dancing in the clubhouse. It's after dark and the place is near-empty, except for the young barmaid staring out from beneath the beer light, sat on a barstool so she can reach the pumps. Her white-hooded sweatshirt glows like a hologram. The room is a mirage of colours, revolving and relaying into each other, a neon spectrum of shapes that overlap the next: jukeboxes, fruit machines, strobes, disco balls. We're trying to trap the lights with our feet as they expand beneath us.

Our parents are drunk. They're in the middle of the floor, slow-dancing; only it's not proper dancing. They're just shuffling from side-to-side in each other's arms, Mum looking up at my Dad. His chin is rested on his chest to meet her gaze. There's a faint smile etched onto his face, an expression I've never seen. Like someone's pulling the corner of his lip with a fishing wire. My mum is smoking, lifting the cigarette up to my dad's lips every so often and then taking it back. The smoke is like a studio effect. I swear, I see a spotlight appear on the dance floor as the bulbs around us dim.

The image is as revelatory as the first time I saw snow falling, an aeroplane landing, the sound of a match day football crowd heaving down a summer street. We're rooted to the spot. I wonder if we've been sucked into the portable TV in the caravan. We're witnessing a movie scene, a transmission from Hollywood-land, only we're part of it. We have our own script, our own roles to play.

THE MATING CALL
OF A FOX

You can hear them go at it after dark. From the sand dunes and the tall reeds on the land behind my room at The Finniland Inn. I lie there thinking, Christ, even the foxes are getting some. The sound is disturbing, like somebody getting their throat slashed. A sound I can relate to: the agony of love.

I unscrew the bulb and stand at the window, scanning for silhouettes. I smoke a cigarette. I try to impersonate the mating call but the animals are wise to it. They never respond.

Every morning the stickers reappear on my car. Across the windshield, the bonnet, the back window. Everything is covered. Takes me an hour to pick them off. The stickers say, *Hunt People, Not Foxes* and are a chemical red that bleed onto the car's paint-work.

I've got no idea why I'm being singled out. Some-body on the island thinks I'm some politician or other, a man of authority, with opinions. They think I'm someone I'm not.

NOT FOR SALE

NOT FOR SALE.

The sign says.

Another sign says, HANDS OFF.

One sign says, YOU BREAK IT, YOU BUY IT.

This other one says YOU CAN'T AFFORD IT, SO SCRAM.

There's a white football shirt hanging in front of a shelf full of comics.

Next to the shirt is a framed photograph of the footballer Paul Gascoigne.

There's a scribbled autograph in felt tip on the shirt.

The sign next to this says TOUCH IT AND I'LL KILL YOU.

These signs are dotted around a shop, believe it or not.

A *shop*.

The shop, called Harry's And Mal's Memorabilia Emporium, or Planet X, is run by two men called Harry and Mal. They opened the shop together after being local rivals for years.

After struggling their way through the early 2000s, they decided it would be easier to pool their stock and sell it under one roof, halving the rent.

They combined the names of their shops, too, unable to agree on one or the other.

Now, inside the shop, they shuffle around each

another like twins in the womb. The psychic spaces they occupy are unspoken and understood. Their territories are marked.

They amuse themselves by playing cruel pranks on each other.

Harry let the tyres down on Mal's original 1954 Austin Champ jeep every day for a year, until Mal had to call British Army engineers out to investigate.

They hoisted it up with a crane, at great cost, but couldn't find a problem.

In revenge, Mal convinced Harry the shop was haunted.

He drew a bloody crucifix on the mirror in his workshop. At night, he hid in the ceiling panels and used a tiny projector to show an old Super 8 home movie of Harry as a child, opening presents on Christmas Day.

Harry was spooked.

He hired an exorcist. A man named Collings came and found there to be a malevolent spirit in the shop, by the name of Lee Blundell.

While Collings worked, Mal hid in the toilet, doubled over with his hand covering his mouth.

He laughed so much he thought he might have to phone an ambulance.

It is a better life now, they would both secretly agree, and not half as lonely.

Harry and Mal's Memorabilia Emporium, or Planet X, is located on the avenues that lie behind the North Parade, the long promenade road where Coral Island's famous pier is.

Mal mainly collects rare coins and war memorabilia. He likes the feel of a WWI trench coat and the smell of a leather canteen from the Vietnam War.

He has Nazi helmets and Imperial Eagle pins. There are real Purple Hearts and Victoria Crosses. There are machetes from the Boer War and signed memoirs of Field Marshal Montgomery.

On his side of the shop, camouflage netting dresses the ceiling and falls down over a glass counter that displays rare medieval coins.

Deep down, Mal doesn't want to sell anything.

He'd like to sit and watch his collection grow until it cocoons him, a sacred palace of stuff.

He has a pension from somewhere or other that Harry doesn't know about. It allows him to buy and sell whatever takes his fancy, without ever having to make a profit.

All of the NOT FOR SALE signs are written in his hand.

Mal is a beachcomber, and when not in the shop you can find him out on the sand at Coral Bay, dutifully raking the dunes, metal detector in hand.

Bloop. Bloop. Bloop.

He is forty-six years old, five feet six inches, balding, and lives off a diet of scampi fries, battered fish and milk.

Comics are Harry's obsession. He started out reading DC and Marvel, like most kids. From there he burrowed deeper, into Steve Ditko's world, rare stuff that he had to save pocket money for.

When he started reading 2000 AD and the British Vertigo imprint, he felt as if someone had taken an axe to his head, letting his imagination escape into the world.

These formative reading years gave Harry the collecting bug.

His side of the shop is filled wall-to-wall with comics, graphic novels, horror masks, baseball bats, football shirts and figurines.

Taking up most space is a huge hand-painted diorama of The Joker escaping from Arkham Asylum.

As collections go, Harry's out-values Mal's.

He frequents the Comic Con events and book signings.

He waits outside tennis and football arenas hoping for players to sign a racket or a ball.

He knows the car boot sales and auctions, and when a certain actor or sportsman is down on his luck and might want to clear out his loft for the right fee.

Some say he has the black leather glove of Tommie Smith, a set of Flo Jo's fingernails, Luis Resto's illegal and tampered with boxing gloves that ended the career of Billy Collins Jr.

Once, he persuaded Christopher Lee to part with a pair of vampire fangs that he wore in the movie *Dracula Has Risen From The Grave.*

Harry knows how to hustle and trade and how to drive down a price.

He is fifty-four years old, six and a half feet tall,

and suffers from acute diabetes.

Today, the Pier is quiet.

It is the first week of September. All the way up and down the promenade, a wind blows. It is an ill wind of empty warehouses and haunted shipyards.

There isn't a soul in sight.

Mal is sulking at the back of the shop, gently rocking in an original Luftwaffe leather cockpit seat, sipping a glass of blue top milk.

Harry is in his workshop, making a note of the day's jobs. There are comics to list, figurines to repair, auctions to bid on.

It's a busy day for Harry.

But like I said, Mal, Mal is sulking.

See, there's one thing that keeps him awake at night.

An obsession.

He lies there in bed, projecting it onto the Artex ceiling.

He thinks about it

He dreams about it.

It is a neon spinning marine.

What?

A neon spinning marine.

Next door to the shop, there is a Laser Quest, an old converted warehouse full of tunnels and sniper points and cushioned trenches.

Kids go in and invent names for their armies. They fight three-hour wars with plastic guns that shoot pinpoint rays of light.

The neon spinning marine is in one of the end zones. It is an army soldier, made from the same light as the guns shoot.

If a team storms another's end zone, the game is over. The neon spinning marine must be defended at all costs.

It is the coveted trophy of the game.

It is life-size, and spins perpetually in slow motion.

Mal saw it one day when he discovered a door leading from his side of the shop into the warehouse.

Since then, he hasn't been able to stop thinking about it.

Harry shouts through to Mal:

"Flick that gas heater on."

"Put it on yourself," Mal says with a scarf around his mouth. "Warm."

"What's up your arse today?"

Mal, in his best sulking voice:

"You know what."

Harry plays dumb. Mal says:

"I want the neon spinning marine."

Harry won't hear it again.

"How many times..."

"I want it."

"It's not real, Mal. It's a trick of the eye..."

Three boys enter the shop. They walk directly over to a rack of oversized German Army coats and combat shirts. They try them on, giggling at themselves in the mirror.

Mal reaches into a desk drawer, picks up a grenade shell, throws it and shouts, "FIRE IN THE HOLE!"

It hits the floor and spins around their feet.

The kids jump and run out of the shop in fits of shocked hysterics.

A telephone rings. Harry takes a call. He notes down an address, says yes three times and hangs up.

He shouts:

"Ray was in before."

Mal perks up.

"Oh yeah?"

"Says she might sell Arcadia. No one's playing the arcades."

Mal says, "I told her about my five pound admission rule... she didn't listen."

"What's that?"

Harry has begun repainting the sailor's cap on the head of a 'Stay Puft' marshmallow man from the Ghostbusters movie.

With the paintbrush, he nudges his spectacles down to the tip of his nose and peers around the partition.

"What's this five pound thing?"

"Like I said: on the arcade machines. Instead of charging, say one pound per go, which skints the kids, you make all the arcades free. Unlimited lives, unlimited credits."

"Explain to me how that works," Harry grumbles.

"Simple. You charge a fiver at the door. Once in, the kids get infinite plays. No coins, no slots."

"You'd never get rid of them."

"It's like the cinema. You make the money on sweets and drinks. Kids can't afford a quid for ten seconds on *Tekken 3*. It's scared them off."

"I can't see it."

"Because you're a tight-arse, Harry."

"My arse."

"Minge-bag."

"Takes one to know one."

Years ago, the comic shops on the North Parade were routinely packed. There'd be overnight queues around the block for signed copies of the new *Hellblazer* or *V For Vendetta, Spawn* figurines that had a limited factory run.

The Internet auction sites changed all that.

Harry and Mal, they'll both tell you. Mal especially. He took the rise of Internet shops personally, a direct affront to the sanctity of his profession.

You get some shyster sitting in their mother's box room somewhere, undercutting everyone, selling everything half price, getting cheese sandwiches brought to them on a stair lift.

Some of us have rent to pay.

The kids are back at the window, making faces. Mal sits there reading, pretending he hasn't seen, scratching his ear with his bird finger raised. It sends the kids back into fits of giggles.

Harry unpacks a stack of comics from a brown UPS box. He hauls them to the top end of the shop by the front door.

For the first time, he sees Mal's note next to the signed Paul Gascoigne football shirt.

He rips it from the wall and shouts, "MAL!", and marches back to Mal's side of the shop.

The sound of a cobbling machine whirrs into existence. Mal begins mending the broken sole of a soldier's boot.

Harry fumes, waving the sign at the back of his head:

"STOP IT WITH THE SIGNS, MAL! How am I supposed to SELL ANYTHING?"

"They don't deserve it," Mal shouts, half-panicked. The cobbling machine is at full pelt, spitting machine-gun salvos. He is hunched over, facing the wall, hiding behind the sound.

Harry has more to say, but it is inaudible over the thud of the presser bar coming down on the boot.

Eventually, Mal grinds the machine to a halt. He sits for a second, facing the wall. Quietly, he mutters:

"They don't deserve us."

"I give up." Harry says, and huffs back to his workshop.

There is a silence that feels like wet concrete.

"Going out for a bite," Mal says, in half-apology.

"Don't choke on a fishbone."

Before I eat, Mal thinks, I'll have a peek. It's only next-door.

In the dark and empty Laser Quest, Mal sleep-walks toward it, guided by fluorescent markers that glow nocturnal.

"I am nothing without it," he whispers to himself.

"I am nothing."

He can taste his perspiration. He feels his heartbeat increase.

It is thrilling.

Up an unlit set of stairs it is there, in its quiet meditation.

Revolving, revolving.

It is made of thousands of illuminated strobes, all
firing in the same direction.

It is on one knee, bayonet rifle pointed out and up
toward the imagined enemy.

It is perfect.

Mal reaches out and tries to touch it.

The beams study his hand like Mal himself was a
ghost, made of nothing but light and air.

He stands there until time slips away, opening and
closing his palm as the light bends and refracts
around him.

From a door at the opposite end of the room, the
sound of advancing footsteps, and the laughter of
children.

HARRY AND MAL

MURIEL & MIRANDA (THE MERMAID TWINS)

They wouldn't lift a finger, the Mermaid Twins.

In the old days, they'd have an assistant each, a gopher, whatever you want to call it, that were glorified servants really, because Muriel and Miranda were more than capable of looking after themselves.

They were geniuses, in fact.

A Mermaid Twin gopher would always be a man of a certain age and build (let's call it *young and athletic*) that the twins called their 'Mermen'.

They designed uniforms for their Mermen: green swimming trunks, golden gloves and a bronze shoulder guard.

Each Merman had a trident strapped to his back.

And the Mermaid Twins would sit there in the mornings, in the middle of the grand aquarium foyer, and smoke and eat and drink Martinis, while their Mermen worked around them.

Muriel and Miranda were born with a condition called Sirenomelia, or Mermaid Syndrome, which meant their legs were fused together at birth.

When the news went around Coral Island, sometime in the late 1920s, people thought it was a bad omen: the pier closed for a week, a Supermoon rose above the sea of Estrangia, and three extra wicker men were commissioned to guard the South East of the Island, the side that's exposed to Rainland, or Great Britain as we know it.

The same month, The Amazing Primo Nition, the Island's most famous psychic, predicted a year of terrible storms that would wreck everything.

That is, until Muriel and Miranda got into the water.

Things changed very rapidly after that.

Against the odds, they were natural swimmers.

Sometimes it was like they were synchronised, or choreographed. They imitated the fluid flight of dolphins and could murmurate with each other. They could do killer whales breaching, and gannets diving at a herring shoal.

The Mermaid Show was a kind of underwater ballet that they had been perfecting since the womb.

Prophet Zaar, the self confessed King of the North Pier and Palace Palladium Ringmaster, declared the birth of Muriel and Miranda a 'miracle of the ages'.

They were turned into stars. You'd see their picture on billboards and cafe walls. They became one of the North Pier's biggest attractions, working seven days a week through twenty-five consecutive summers.

In time they grew to resent being one of the island's hottest tickets.

It was like an albatross around their neck.

They'd go missing for days. Miranda would fall into trances in which she claimed to be speaking to the spirits of dead sailors, or *draugens,* and these spirits told her that the water in the North Pier Aquarium was from the Sea of Estrangia, and cursed.

There were other vagaries to their personalities.

Both twins talked in their sleep. They'd sleep talk in Chinese. Muriel was convinced that they were connected to the ancient Chinese dragons Feilong and Huáng Lóng.

When the aquarium temporarily shut down in the 1970s, Prophet Zaar re-branded them as The Amazing Dragon Sisters, but it failed to catch on. Muriel couldn't take to the trapeze and Miranda missed her Mermen.

They moved down to the South Pier, where they were welcomed with open arms.

They wanted to turn their backs on everything and start afresh.

Muriel opened a brothel called 'Norwegian Wood', and became the Madam there for twenty years, before it was torched in an insurance job that went right.

Miranda, a cinema fanatic, poured every penny she had into a movie production company.

The films she produced were English language, but she insisted on them having English subtitles, so they appeared more 'art-house'. They had names like *A Mermaid in Paris, The Immaculate Pearl Divers, Fifty Fathoms Deep,* and *A Nightmare on North Pier,* all of them flops.

MERMAID TWINS

OVER CORAL ISLAND

If you stare at the Wonder Wheel long enough -
I mean *really stare*.

Then for the rest of the day you'll see skeletons imprinted on your eyeballs. We'll do it for hours, me and Connie.

And all day we'll be singing, the knee-bone's connected to the thigh-bone.

There's this shop, right. It's called Harry and Mal's something or other, but everyone calls it Planet X.

It sells allsorts.

It sells comics and knives and old gas masks that look like ghosts from a war.

One of the owners is called Harry. He asks us to keep our eye out for bits and bobs around the car boot sales and the charity shops and that.

He says to us, them old WWF wrestling figures are selling. Look for some of these: British Bulldog, Jake The Snake Roberts, Brett Hart.

See how you go.

So we'll switch our internal radars on, our spid-ey-sense, and go out looking.

If we have to steal once or twice then so be it.

We come back to Harry at teatime when he's closing up.

He'll bring us into his workshop that smells of

Turps and Nitromorse and old newspaper.

What have you boys got for me?

We'll empty rucksacks out into his workbench and he'll study things with a magnifier:

Worthless reissue... bad condition... little nick on the ... oh hang on, this looks promising.

If there's something that takes his fancy he'll offer us this or that or a bit of money but we'll say no Harry, you know what we want.

Yeah Harry, you know what we want.

We want the Boston Primer.

Yeah we want the Boston Primer, Harry.

The model paint.

Two tins please, chief.

The best spot is out on the rocks past Finniland. Nobody goes there.

You get the lapping of the waves and the salt air laced with the faintest spin so every gust is like a refresher.

Behind you the charred and abandoned beach homes stare like the crooked smiles of circus drivers.

We get old dishrags and soak them in the Boston Primer.

You have to wait for a bit 'til it releases, then put it over your nose and you huff.

In two minutes flat you feel it.

The rest of the day I drift over Coral Island, weightless as a chair-o-plane, high up, higher than Holy Joe's radio tower.

I can see the caravan sprawl and the light from the

wreck of The Arklow. I can see people on the board-walks, happy people, and the fairs beaming their splendour out to the world.

Everything is good up here, over Coral Island.

It's all a sea, a great shining sea, an imagination of itself.

I think about the afterlife, where Mum lives. How money and possessions are meaningless there, and the only thing you take with you is your freedom.

Up here I know, I just know I am as free on these great piers as I will be on the next.

THE VISITORS

I can't quite describe the feeling I get when I think back to that night, or how we ended up out there on the outskirts of Coral Island.

We were way back behind the container port, where the streets haven't been regenerated since the twenties, and the old tenement buildings jut out of the cobbles like drunk scarecrows.

It was a weeknight, Wednesday I think, and we only stumbled into that lopsided pub because it had started hailing volleys of ice the size of our fists, and the wind was blowing a hoolie.

On our way in, Joey-O called this pub The Leaning Tower of Pilsner.

Earlier, we'd meant to go and see a band, but the Happy Al's bus that we'd meant to catch to the concert venue had broken down, so we decided to hop the last ferry to Coral Island, to continue whatever misadventure this fluke of events had gifted us. And besides, we could drink up there on the top deck, gliding across the great silver waterway.

We jumped off at the secondary ferry port and saw the bright magical North Pier in the distance.

But we were a long way from there. That's when the hail started, and we saw the pub.

To get inside, we walked under a staircase, paid a couple of quid, and a man stamped our hands with the emblem of a white star.

The band were well into their set by the time we arrived, and the small room was heaving.

We thought it must have been used as a spice warehouse once, because it smelled of turmeric and damp burlap; there were the scents of heavy stouts too, and sweet smoke from a high wooden mezzanine.

Immediately, the sound from the small stage at the back of the room stopped us dead. It was definitely our thing, that is to say, guitar music with melodies, hints of The Byrds, The Everly Brothers, all that stuff.

But there were other things in there: the rhythm of runaway trains, faint reverberations from an older, stranger time. Don't get me wrong, they weren't one of those fancy-dress retro affairs; they were rooted absolutely in the now.

They looked perfect too, like characters from that book *The Outsiders*.

What really captivated us was something about the pain in the singer's voice - not in a self-indulgent way - the opposite really, a sort of blue-eyed defiance against the world. And the notes he hit. Every line, every syllable was its own life story, a million miles of experience.

He couldn't have been older than twenty-three. There were five in the band, like the old beat groups, and that's the way they played, I think, in that haunted way, the Eddie Cochran or Cramps way, but some kind of sad maritime thread running through everything, every song interlocking, as intense and precise as clockwork.

We watched, me and Joey-O, we watched in silence, because we were transfixed.

And outside while we were having a smoke, we got speaking to a girl called Karen who'd been following them from the beginning.

She told us that they sometimes played in the gargantuan hulls of old shipping freighters.

Once there'd been some kind of séance, although she didn't go into too much detail because there were lads there I'd seen at the South Pier before this, and that would be something a goth would say, not this crowd, who I guessed were more of a scally pier gang who did speed, dabbled in acid every now and again.

Anyway, Karen said, the lead singer, he's fucking full of himself and he thinks he's *psychic.*

After the encore, we stumbled outside looking for a way home.

Everything around us was amplified, biblical almost; the silhouette of an old submarine in a dry dock, a turreted building that looked like the Tower of Babel.

Joey-O agrees with me to this day, as far-fetched as it all sounds. We were completely sucked in.

On my way out I'd grabbed a flyer advertising the band's next thing, a festival on the other side of the island near one of the big parks. Strangely though, I couldn't find a trace of them. I looked everywhere. I asked around all the piers and pubs, the cellar-room record shops and arcades, but people either drew a blank, or were covering up for them, as if it was some secret that nobody wanted to blow the lid off.

I didn't think I'd ever hear of them again, until now. Here it is, in my hand, in this Cash Converters store, twenty years later, the cassette bootleg of that very gig, right down to the exact date.

And I can hear them again, those songs, and I'm almost crying as I write.

A NIGHT AT THE CALICO GIRL

THE LIGHTNING TREE

THE LIGHTNING TREE

Gray caught the bus early that day, because, whether he liked it or not, his hollow woke him up, and when his hollow talked, every bit of his body listened. There was no other choice.

It wasn't a sound as such, more of a feeling that he could see and hear and touch and smell.

A *hollow*.

True, there were parts of Gray that ached. They ached because of the shipping warehouse he worked nights in. He'd drive the forklift, stack palettes, load cargo.

But aches could always be healed, and Gray knew how to sleep away an ache. He was good at sleeping. He slept for a whole weekend once, and woke feeling hungry and refreshed, ready to take on the world.

There were parts of him that yearned. They yearned because he had never really met anyone he could say he'd loved or been intimate with.

Of course, there were people he'd had infatuations for, but they had mostly led him down a dead-end of stuttered conversations and long days of stalking in the rain.

But anyway, spending a day with his mum could always allay the yearning: washing her hair, fetching her arthritis medicine.

There were parts of him that wondered. They wondered because the furthest he'd ever been outside of his tiny hometown of Carham was when his mum took him 'abroad' to the Isle of Man once when he was eight. He'd caught meningitis there and had to be airlifted to hospital.

But after a while, the wondering would subside. He could lose himself in things. He loved maps. He loved the map of Coral Island most, and the North Pier, which he had never seen in real life, but dreamed about a lot.

It was the part of him that was hollow, the part way down in the pit of his stomach that concerned him most.

This hollow, this strange feeling of drifting through time and space was the thing that kept him awake at night.

He felt like an oil barrel from a scrapyard, bobbing along on a great and endless ocean.

The more it went on, he could feel himself beginning to rust.

So Gray woke that morning feeling hollow, but with a determination to try and fill the chasm in his soul.

Only last week he'd seen a leaflet fly posted to the South Pier boardwalk entrance. It was raining and the ink had run slightly, but he could still make the words out:

'Celestial Congregation of The
Lightning Tree Children have a
brand new home! Come to 345
Trinity Lodge, Parkgate Bluffs,
Coral Island.
We're new here, so say hello!'

Gray pulled the poster from the wall and pocketed it.

At night, he'd study it. There was a photograph of a huge tree, which was completely white. Only the trunk of the tree remained. There were no branches, just a single white trunk shooting up to the sky like a magician's finger.

Who were the Lightning Tree Children, and what did they want from him?

On the bus, Gray sat and listened to his favourite songs. He'd tape them from a radio show he liked called Holy Joe's Rock n' Roll Medicine Show. The show was broadcast all across the island from a big silver tower.

He listened to *Never Go Home Anymore* by The Shangri-Las.

He listened to *Runaway* by Del Shannon.

He listened to *Mr Moonlight* by The Beatles (the old, weird Beatles).

He listened to *Rollercoaster By The Sea* by Jonathan Richman.

He played a game on his phone called *Devious Dungeon.*

In the game, a man was trapped in a basement full of monsters. Each time one touched him it would peel away a piece of his armour, like a spaulder or chain mail vest.

After that, he ate a sandwich and fell asleep.

When he woke, the bus was passing a place called Caravan City, which is a whole valley filled with static trailers and holiday homes. There were so many that Gray couldn't imagine how many there were. The number that came into his head was a gazillion.

There was a huge generator that spewed out black smoke. Gray guessed that this powered the whole place. It was getting worked pretty hard, he thought.

The bus terminated at a town called Finniland, which is where the leaflet said Gray needed to be.

As they pulled in, a man wearing a sandwich board was standing in the middle of the road. The board said:

LIVE-EVIL
LIVED-DEVIL
DOG-GOD
GOD-DOG
DELIVER-REVILED

He was holding a bunch of daffodils, shaking them first at his face then down at his knee, like an African shaman. The bus had to swerve to miss him.

The engine purred to a standstill.

Before he got off the bus, Gray thanked the driver.

He stood in the station forecourt, wondering what to do.

A girl was in the waiting area. She wore a rucksack, denim shorts and walking boots. Her hair was done in tight bunches and there was a daffodil painted under one eye.

Gray had a feeling.

"Um..." he said, walking toward her. "Scuseme."

The girl was reading the leaflet that Gray had

pulled from the South Pier wall.

"Hi!" she said, smiling. She noticed Gray was holding the same leaflet she was.

"You're going there too? Let's walk." She held her phone up and shook it.

"I've got the address on Google maps."

"I'm Elena," Elena said, holding out her hand.

"Gray," Gray said.

The suburbs of Finniland were pretty strange. The houses were old and rotted. There were some that didn't have windowpanes. Some had half a roof missing. Others looked like they'd been beaten up. One had been charred by fire, and black soot spewed out of windows and up the front wall like nightmare snakes.

The odd thing was, all of the houses had people living in them. New cars sat on overgrown driveways. Underwear waved from long washing lines. It was like a whole load of people had descended on a ghost town and made it a town-town again.

Gray and Elena crabbed along an unnamed street.

Elena liked to talk.

Elena told him about her gap year in Bali, her horses. She told him about her first time trying cocaine, her school friends.

She told him about her annoying dad, the stockbroker, and how he made her feel a certain way, kind of an emptiness, almost like a hollow.

But by this point, Gray had switched off. Elena's voice had become white noise.

Something else had grabbed his attention.

On the windowsill of each house, there were little flashing figurines of a man.

The man's arms were by his side. His palms were facing outwards, the way Jesus is commonly depicted. But Gray thought it couldn't be Jesus because the figure was overweight, had hair like Bon Jovi, wore black wraparound sunglasses and had an earring.

When Elena had almost finished telling Gray her life story, Gray cut her short by saying, "We're here."

Inside the Lightning Tree mansion, Gray and Elena were ushered into a narrow hallway by a woman wearing a lightning bolt badge pinned to the breast of her trouser suit.

The woman told Gray and Elena to sit, and someone would attend to them shortly.

Everything in the hallway was colour-coded in black, white and purple.

There were strange trinkets on tables: an ornate seafaring compass. A small gin bell that was made completely of jade. Framed medical diagrams hung from walls.

There were many doors that led to other rooms. Gray could hear people talking, and the low whirr of machinery.

He wondered about the Lightning Tree.

From behind a desk in front of them, a man was talking on the phone. He spoke in a low, secretive voice. You could hear the moisture on his lips:

"Unarmed combat... Oriental philosophies...

some, not all... no money needed... cheap as chips... natural land detoxified... Jackson the... he dreams... cancers and virile flus halved within a week... addicts free from withdrawal... follicle extraction... no, not like him."

The man hadn't yet noticed that they were there.

Gray stood up and decided to look in one of the closed rooms.

He went to a door, pushed it open and peered in.

He saw a bare room with a black and white tiled floor.

At the far end of the room there was a topless woman holding a pair of scissors and a comb. She was stood at the head of a large torpedo-shaped contraption, which Gray recognised as an iron lung.

The person inside the iron lung was having their hair cut.

Snip snip. Whirr.

The breathing machine inhaled and exhaled with robotic bursts of pressure. Gray suddenly noticed the unconscious mechanism of his own lungs. In, out, in...

The receptionist's voice made him jump.

"Okay! I'm sorry those rooms are private."

Gray closed the door and went back to his seat.

The man hung the phone up, smiled and slotted his fingers between the other, like a thatched roof.

"Let's have your bags taken to your chalets. Then you can meet Odeon. Yes? Who wants to meet Odeon?"

Who was Odeon, Gray wondered.

*   *   *

"And they persecuted us to within an inch of our lives. So fuck it, we thought. Let's move on. And then I heard about Coral Island and just thought to myself, y'know. This place is perfect."

Odeon was giving Gray and Elena a tour of the grounds.

Behind the crumbling shabby mansion there was a small village of caravans, corrugated chalets and tents.

He walked ahead without once looking back, strangling a crooked roll-up cigarette between his teeth.

Odeon spoke in a kind of transatlantic American-English accent that couldn't decide which side of the pond it belonged on.

Gray knew Odeon as the man depicted in the neon figurines: tall and confident. The way he held himself was certainly Christ-like, but with a whiff of the used car salesman. The wraparound sunglasses were there, the mane of hair, the earring, and one gold tooth that flashed when he spoke, like a lie.

Gray saw that Elena was already transfixed by, and possibly in love with, Odeon.

Further on, he noticed that they were now holding hands.

Odeon told them about The Lightning Tree. Come see it, he said.

While they walked, people peered from behind the curtains of the chalets and trailers. Children ran out and then ran back again, like it was a spy game.

All the people wore the same clothes: grey gym socks pulled to the knee, grey pumps, short-shorts, and a long, washed out purple shirt that hung down to their calves at the back, but stopped at their waist at the front. Printed on the front of the shirt was a circle with a lightning bolt inside.

Everybody also wore a type of bindi, a tiny purple lightning bolt on the forehead, between the eyebrows.

They ventured around a long caravan, over a culvert, to a fenced area.

Odeon ushered them into it.

In the dead centre was a tall tree, the tallest Gray had ever seen.

There were no branches on the tree, just one thin, long trunk that was shock white, and a bed of gnarled roots at the bottom that little capillaries and rivulets of silver ran through.

Elena started laughing. She jumped up and down, and clapped her hands. Gray thought she was over-doing it a little.

Odeon explained that The Lightning Tree had been uprooted from their last commune, on The Mull of Kintyre, in Scotland. A man named McCartney had them evicted with JCB diggers and relentless bagpipe music that went on through the night.

Odeon described it as *musical terrorism*.

The tree had been alive for thousands of years he said, and travelled the breadth of Europe, in whatever home The Children had found for it.

It could heal the body, as well as the mind, and the most devout worshippers experienced an awakening of the human 'third eye', the psychic eye.

The tree was constantly bathed in neon indigo. Odeon said that the tree produced its own light that no scientist could find the source of.

But you'll learn all about that tomorrow in the first 'healing' session, Odeon said, which was called 'Fullfillingness in the Aura of our Receptor'.

He explained that it was important he and Elena stay close to the tree tonight.

Next to it, Gray did feel a sense of belonging, a feeling in him that he could only describe as *the weight of knowledge*, as if something in him had been rebooted, or awakened.

Elena was looking at him with tears in her eyes, nodding, like she felt it too.

Odeon hugged Gray, then Elena.

When he hugged Elena, Odeon cupped his hands around her buttocks.

"You're going to be so happy here," he said.

That night, Gray couldn't settle.

The chalet was comfortable enough: clean sheets, a nice bed and a shower with different heat settings.

Still, he felt uneasy.

He looked in the mirror and played with the lightning bolt that Odeon had placed on his forehead earlier.

He unfolded the leaflet from his pocket and lay in bed.

There was something he hadn't read before, on the back, in tiny lettering. It said:

'Visitors will only be billed IF
enlightenment is achieved
(subject to review by Odeon), in
which case a total fee of £249.99
will be charged, followed by 9
extra monthly charges of £69.70'

Gray went to the window.

The light from the Lightning Tree was going on and off, blinking in perfect time, like the ticking hand of a clock.

It was like it was sending him a message.

He went out to investigate.

Under the tree, the blinking indigo light was strangely hypnotic.

High up, a star moved across the sky very gently, as if it were pulling a black hole toward the moon. Gray tracked its trajectory until he was facing the opposite direction.

There was a noise.

It coincided with the blinking of the tree. The noise sounded like the squeaking of a gate, if the gate was out of breath.

Gray followed the noise round to the underground culvert at the back end of the tree.

He went into it, the sound becoming clearer now.

Huh-ah-huh-ah-huh-ah.

What was it?

Elena's rucksack, half in the shallow stream water.

Then, Odeon, on his knees.

They were entwined with one another, naked, the curves of their body clear in the dimmet, like negative silhouettes.

For some reason, Gray fixated on Odeon's socks, which were the only things on him.

One of them was a grey, over washed gym sock, while the other was a woman's black fishnet, with frills at the cuff.

Gray could see the outline of him, his milkwhite saggy arse turning a small wall switch on and off as he thrust his hips in and out.

Gray knew then that this was where the power supply for the tree was.

It was blinking in time with their rhythm.

He couldn't believe what he was seeing.

He didn't remember much after that, except that he ran.

He ran so far and fast that he blacked out, and when he came to, he was riding the night bus.

His arms were bleeding from the birch of twigs and dense bracken.

He was many miles away from The Lightning Tree, but he was in a place he recognised.

Gray looked around.

The bus was empty, except for him and a man

wearing a denim jacket with dirty white wings sewn into the back, and a yellow Tennis headband that told him to Just Do It.

The man was getting off the bus. When he walked, his head stayed very still, as if he was gliding.

Gray followed.

As soon as he stepped off he was filled with a rush of warmth that made his fingertips tingle and his toes curl.

He felt it wash from one ear to the other, like a divine river.

Most of all, he felt the warmth fill up his gut, and where his hollow once was now felt like a great dam swelling with rainwater.

He was at Coral Island North Pier.

He saw the elegant and otherworldly spotlights of the boardwalk and the Palace Palladium, stretching out into Coral Bay.

He saw the celestial beams from the super aquarium, the amusements and the wondrous new casino. Cable cars went to and fro in the high sky, like the true trajectory of angels. People walked hand in hand, lost in a dream of each other.

Gray realised that he had had discovered it, his god.

It had been in front of him all along, the thing that would finally get rid of his hollow.

ODEON

Finniland Song Of The Lightning Tree

(trad arr)

Forget my face, my history
Now I am just a memory
Happiness is certainly
inside the lightning tree
inside the lightning tree

Doh - ray - mee, A-B-C,
I'm enlightened as can be
And this is my song to thee
Come find the lightning tree
Come find the lightning tree

RUNNING WITH THE DOGS

We are the Wolfpack of Coral Island South Pier.

We are the alleyway Alsatians, the marauding mongrels.

We are one-eyed, mange-infected, limp-legged, flea-bitten and rejected.

We are stray.

We are our own masters.

We live on candyfloss scraps and popcorn seeds.

We are the dregs of society, the bottom of the barrel, the true guttersnipes.

We don't do tricks.

We are foul mouthed, hated by everyone and we *love it*.

Take your bow-wows, woof-woofs, heel, paw, sit, fetch, and stick them you-know-where.

People think we don't notice what goes on.

For instance, we know Price's Plastic Surgeon uses margarine for their lip filler. You see women stepping out of the front door like stitched princesses, pristine and bruised, mouths puffed out like duck's beaks.

Days later, the margarine filler has gone flat and they're sitting there with faces like a burst casey.

And what about Daley the grifter who spends

hours in the bookies, feeding money into the fruit machines and taking punts on greyhound races in places as far away as Belize?

He'll lose a week's earnings in a single afternoon.

He'll come out drunk, headbutt a lamppost, and then punch himself in the nose so his wife thinks he's been mugged.

You see the weightlifting types, the boys with the big arms and little dingalings. They smuggle steroids into their fish finger sandwiches at the Marine Diner.

And what about the new wave machine that's been installed in the Suncentre? People are losing their minds over it. They're walking around in Bermuda shorts with surfboards under their arms, quoting Miki Dora.

Apparently it's the biggest wave ever made. People are flying in from all over the world just to surf it. They had to remove the roof of the building so the wave didn't rip through.

A bloodhound who runs with us called Lottie sussed it.

Lottie used to sniff out harmful chemicals when there'd been a fire at a laboratory or a pharmaceutical factory.

One day she saw armoured trucks with hazardous warnings on the side of them. They were going into the basement entrance of the Suncentre.

She caught the scent straight away.

Lottie thinks they're using uranium to create the wave. That's the same element they use for the atom bomb.

We chased after the trucks and barked at them, but two security guards ran out and beat us with sticks and cattle prods. It took a whole month for some of us to recover. I don't know why we bothered.

The only person who's nice to us is a strange woman called Brenda Broad who works for the council. She goes around with a camera strapped to her breast handing out fines to people who spit chewing gum out on the floor, or throw their ciggy butts away.

She'll always come to Scruff Alley, which is where we sleep. She'll throw us treats, give us bones and bottles of Newcastle Brown, which is our favourite.

She's fixated with this dog we hang around with called Gary.

One night she took Gary to a fancy restaurant. Hired out the whole place. She popped a little bow tie over his head and sat him upright in a chair.

Gary went along with it because he could smell the Ribeye steaks sizzling away behind him in the kitchen.

She gave him a red rose and read him a poem. She fed him slices of steak from her fork.

When they'd finished their food, Brenda Broad leaned over and tried to kiss Gary, and that's when Gary ran.

When we go back to our den we have a right laugh about the humans, the sad cases, the desperate ones.

They think they're better than us when they're just as bad, if not worse.

And what's their problem? We're all on the same ghost train, heading toward the long black tunnel, aren't we? It makes no sense.

We know everybody's secrets. We keep them close to our chest.

One day, we might tell someone.

JONO

Sometimes this thing jumps on my back. Like a bogeyman, or a bad spirit.

I can feel it digging in: its long black talons and blue tongue bring me out in the pale fever.

I call the spirit Barbarossa after a cartoon I read in the paper once.

Other people might know it as the *weight of the fucking world.*

As a young man I set the record for tent hoisting, which is a gypsy contest that most people look down on. But it brings together all the old circus families from miles around. It's a prestige thing.

We go at it for two days in a field somewhere.

There are bloody noses and black eyes and every so often the glint of metal. The winner gets a box-fresh carousel or an HGV straight off the line.

Yeah, I won my first one age eighteen. I won five more in a row after that.

You could say it's my speciality.

Anyway, that's how I built the fair up.

When Dad inherited it from the Bostock family, it was a ruin. The only thing that worked was a punching machine that was full of old pig intestines. Everything else was crocked.

So me, Dad, my friends Kip and Tiny the Giant, we got to work. We shed some blood, I can tell you.

Dad drove us pretty hard, but we made it work.

When Dad's lungs packed in, I became the boss.

They say it's easier nowadays, what with SatNav and the hoisting cranes, and the health and safety.

But you have to work twice as hard at the fair. How are you gonna impress some kid who's come from an eight-hour session on *Call of Duty* or *Fortnite*?

People these days: they're spoilt, over-entertained.

Mum passed over to the Land of The Lost soon after she had the twins.

She'd been sick for a while. The trauma of a forty-eight hour birth, her body never recovered.

She made me make some promises up there on the top floor of St. Anne's.

One was that we'd never tell the boys how she went, and I'll take that to my own grave.

A promise is a promise.

Not long after, I met Tammy on the boardwalk.

There've been others before Tammy but none like her. She's got this way of seeing things.

Tammy used to escort the rich old bachelors around the North Pier, laugh at their jokes, whatever.

I'd see her in the early hours. We'd go to this club called Flat Foot Sam's. There's a single bowling lane in there, and a red room at the back.

She smokes the Rare Nepalese Chalice, which she gets from Old Chinatown.

Then I started smoking the Rare Nepalese Chalice, which I get from Old Chinatown.

We're a match made in heaven.

It's the only thing that keeps him quiet, the one who brings me down, him, who jumps up onto my back and digs his claws in, the one I call Barbarossa.

JODY AND THE KID

Jesus Christ, Jody is thinking.

She's in the arcade, stood with her arms folded at the mechanical horseracing machine.

This kid.

This kid's win ratio is incredible.

Whatever her system is, she's got the whole thing cracked. She doubles my money, every time.

Every single *time*.

Tuesday morning, nine A.M. without fail, Jody arrives at the kid's house.

Her dad ushers her out of the terrace door without saying hello or goodbye to Jody, reserving his only salutation for his daughter.

His daughter, not Jody's.

He lets the kid sag school that day because it's P.E. in the afternoon, and she won't take to sports.

The thought of the changing rooms, the communal showers, the long pitches of frozen AstroTurf, they make her so anxious she gets ill in the night. She dreams a lot, her dad says, intense dreams, in which she experiences all the senses.

The dreams she has about school distress her the most.

So why force her, he thinks. It's not the Dark Ages. And besides, Jody and the kid have known each other since she was a nipper. They get on. The kid looks up to her.

He himself spoke highly of Jody once, too, but that ship sailed a long time ago.

Still, he knows Jody cares about the kid enough that she wouldn't put her in danger.

That sound:

It still gives Jody butterflies.

It's like an electric fizz, rising up to the top of a bottle. It comes from somewhere deep in the belly of the machine. The feeling in her stomach mirrors its crescendo.

The long room Jody and the kid are in, called Arcadia, is a beachfront relic; its peeling sky-blue and white facade is earmarked for demolition. It will make way for a modern Genting Casino they say, with virtual roulette and croupiers from Rainland, who know the lingo.

Jody looks around.

The place is deserted, save for a few old women, sat like nesting geese beneath huge Egyptian frescos. They stare out of the window toward the sea, flicking ash into tinfoil flying saucers.

The loners are here, the afternoon low-rollers, their half-drunk cans balanced on top of video games and penny pushers.

The place is a loser's paradise.

But the kid, Jody remembers. The kid just won again.

On cue, a second sound comes, a more thrilling one again: coins dropping down into a plastic collection tray.

Clunk. Clunk. Clu-clu-cluuuu....

And so on.

It is the icing on the cake of a perfect run. Today, every bet has been a winner.

The kid looks up at Jody now, smiling, and Jody claps and says hooray, well done.

Inside, she is so happy she could cry.

While the kid plays, Jody is mindful not to get too close. She'll position her next to another adult to make it seem as if she's tagging along while the adult plays the Snakes and Ladders.

If she were seen here, she doesn't like to think what he'd do to her.

Not this time.

Jody might catch herself in the reflective rim of a penny pushing machine and cringe at herself, her thin, painted-on eyebrows, the hair not quite pulled tight enough to her scalp, the stud above her top lip which hovers there like a broken bauble.

All her life, she dressed down.

An arcade worker in a blue cap walks across the patterned floor. Very carefully, he carries two plastic cups overflowing with two pence pieces like they are 99 cones, melting in the sun.

He eyes her suspiciously. The kid shouldn't be in here.

Jody leans over and places five more pound coins in the kid's palm, keeping her gaze fixed on the attendant.

One more bet.

That'll do it.

The four miniature mechanical horses stutter backwards, back to the starting gates.

The kid is leaned on the glass viewing counter, her nose pressed against it.

The horse racing machine is called 'Whittaker's 200 Guineas', and Jody likes it because she thinks the gods are with it. Don't ask her why, or what that means. Her rituals are complex, and without reason.

The kid puts five quid in the slot.

From four options of red, green, white or blue, she bets on the white jockey, which pays out ten times the stake.

It wins by a hair's breadth.

When the machine gives out the maximum return, it sounds to Jody like warplanes blanket-bombing an entire city, a blitzkrieg of pure victory.

She runs to the machine and fills the pockets of her bomber jacket with golden nuggets, scooping them out quicker than they can fall.

She picks the kid up and spins her around. The noise the machine makes is like a submarine torpedo alarm.

Stop, stop, the kid's saying.

The man in the cap is here.

He is flanked by a taller man, dressed in black. He holds a Walkie-Talkie the size of a breezeblock.

Jody sets the kid down.

"Out," Cap Man says, hitching his thumb.

There's a morning train they get.

The kid sits opposite Jody, and swings her feet to the train's stuttered rhythm, as it halfmoons from Carham, up past The Dips and around The Forest of Dreams.

They look out at the gypsy fair being set up, the low-loaders and the cherry pickers and the canvas tent laid out flat like an artificial sea in the middle of the grass.

The kid points out the big lorries with colourful circus insignia painted on the side:
MR BOSTOCK'S BIG TOP OF WONDER.

There's a magical point where, even in November, the air outside fills with dandelion floats and they hang their hands out of the window.

Jody tells her that if you catch them right they become wishes, and wishes become real if you keep them safe and sacred under your bed.

The kid's room is full of them.

The train trundles into the South Pier station, which, on a deserted winter weekday, is as perfect a place as any to while away an afternoon, while the sea moans and the faded glamour of the picture-house plays movies to empty seats.

The other thing that Jody likes is that the machines have better odds down here, and the fruitys aren't rigged like they are in the North.

And besides, if it's the kid playing the machines then it's not really her who's betting, is it?

Sometimes, on the train, she'll look down and open her hand.

In her palm, a brown plastic coin has a gold star in the middle.

Around the rim it says, ONE DAY AT A TIME.

Outside on the promenade, the sky is drowsy; a liver-ticked dog with the Moon in its jaws. Freighters amble around the sea wall toward the North Pier container port.

"Your dad used to sit me on his knee over there," Jody tells the kid, pointing toward a shelter.

They walk over to it.

She picks up a Styrofoam tray with half a portion of chips left in.

"Watch this," Jody says, holding it above her head.

An army of seagulls appear, swooping fearlessly at the tray. Jody shuts her eyes and rides it out, smiling while the kid is in hysterics. They almost tear her to pieces.

When the last seagull has flown away, the kid reaches up toward the chip paper and asks for one.

I'll take her to Wimpy.

There's this recurring dream that the kid calls Dare of the Haunted Horse.

She always dreams it on a Tuesday, after the arcade.

There's a wild horse, with glowing green eyes, and the only way you can lasso it is with a green-eyed snake whip, and when you catch it, the dare is to ride it.

"That right?" Jody says, breaking a cookie in half.

The kid wrestles her jaws around a burger.

"Yup."

"Did you ever catch it?" Jody asks.

The kid says no, but in the dream, Jody does, and she rides it off the South Pier into the sea. But before she goes underwater, she comes back for her and her dad.

Jody dreams her own picture of the haunted horse. She is jockeying it around a track. There is a crowd cheering from a grandstand, and a huge trophy full of gold coins.

She hurdles a fence and shouts giddyup three or four times then throws the horsewhip at the horse's evil owner, who is stood trackside in a Panama hat.

The kid is still talking, but Jody is lost to a world of podiums and betting slips and the thrills of the gamble.

Outside, the wind blows a parasol into the restaurant window. It makes a thud like the Moon falling out of the sky. The parasol somersaults and disappears over the roof.

Jody says to the kid:

"Remember, what do we say to Dad?"

The kid rolls her eyes and says, "We did the sea wall and the crazy golf, then we went to Wimpy AND WE DIDN'T GO NEAR THE ARCADES."

"That's right," Jody says, sipping her drink. "We didn't go near the arcades."

On the way back to the train station, they pass a chip shop called The South Kowloon. There're two on the island: one down here and one on the North

Parade.

Outside it, a crowd of women have gathered with their babies. They scatter around a nearby boating lake, talking to each other, rocking prams that their children sleep in. Halos of bright light surround their heads. They smile down devoutly at their children like caricatures from Catholic prayer cards, unaffected by the quickening wind.

Jody feels a sudden and deep connection to the kid. She says:

"Do full Moon."

The kid lifts her hand up to Jody's. They share the same semi-circular birth mark on the purlicue of opposite hands. When they put them together, the two shapes make a circle, like a full Moon.

Dark now, and past Arcadia again.

Something is happening.

A group of lads are in the foyer. They have barricaded themselves behind the double doors. The security guard who ejected Jody and the kid earlier is banging on the glass, trying to get back in.

Jody recognises some of the lads as the gang she kicked around with last summer, the Grey Harpoons.

Dempsey is there, and Joe Nearly, Gold with his bright mane of hair, Hadlin and Jackie Boy. Their scrambler bikes are parked in the bays outside the ten-pin bowling.

The sight of them makes her smile. They're having a good time.

Jody suddenly clutches at her pockets full of money, and thinks she might come back and join them later if she drops the kid off in time.

Yes, that's what she'll do.

She remembers last Christmas.

It was a Tuesday like any other, except that Jody felt luckier than usual. It was before she had discovered the kid's winning streak.

She had butterflies in her stomach, and there was a clear vision of her future, one that she could see and feel, as if it were playing out in front of her.

Jody had bet everything she had on a slot called Billion Dollar Brain. She went through a hundred quid in under an hour.

The kid was in tears. She didn't understand why they couldn't play the machines any more. Jody knew it too: there's nothing worse for a kid than being in an arcade with no money.

She walked the kid up and down the South Pier, in shock, until it was time for the train.

On their way to the station, they passed the pavilion. They were showing a Christmas pantomime: Peter Pan, if she remembers right. An actor from a TV soap was in it.

It must have been the intermission, because a couple of the cast were in the alleyway having a smoke, still in costume.

That's what Jody remembers most about that day: Tinkerbell outside the theatre on roller skates, dabbing speed onto her tongue, and the kid watching, transfixed, as if she might suddenly up and fly away.

PROPHET ZAAR AND THE HAPPINESS MACHINE

Colonel Edward Fear, or Prophet Zaar as he was later known, was the ringmaster of Coral Island Pier Palace, and the island's most recognised face.

If you've ever been to the island, you'll have seen or heard of him, or both.

He's old now, but his legacy is everywhere.

There are some things about him you might not know.

For example, when we were kids, the rumour went around that Colonel Edward Fear wasn't a real Colonel.

He was a chemical scientist, in fact. In a previous existence, he'd worked in the pharmaceutical trade, for a company called Squibb.

He was a leader in his field. So much so that he was headhunted by the Army. He went to work for them over on Rainland, or Great Britain as they call it.

The Army wanted Edward *Fear* to create a drug that would make their soldiers *fearless*. Can you believe that?

What he loved most about the job was his access to top-secret military files. He'd obsess over the Philadelphia Experiment and the disappearances at The Bermuda Triangle.

He gave himself the title of Colonel because he aspired to a greatness he felt the world hadn't granted him yet.

He had everything, except for that.

One day, in the course of his research, Edward Fear happened on a chemical compound mixture that had a strange effect:

It made him happy.

It made other people happy, too.

He walked around the laboratory, placing test tubes of it on the desks of unsuspecting assistants and secretaries.

After three or four minutes, they'd be smiling.

Ten minutes in and they'd be hugging one another, tears of joy in their eyes.

They'd talk about donating their worldly belongings to charity, or how they were moving to Africa to save the elephants.

Fear took it outdoors, to the public.

He'd walk around the old North Pier, testing it out.

The results excited him.

Around this time, Edward Fear began to change.

He started to call himself 'Prophet Zaar', and called his chemical mixture 'The Happiness Machine.'

Prophet Zaar was an extension, or exaggeration of Edward Fear's personality.

Another thing was, he'd become interested in the

occult.

He'd started to practice necromancy, communicating with the dead, that sort of thing.

He'd stare into a great glowing ball and pretend to talk to Ghengis Khan and the great emperor, Julius Caesar.

People began to notice.

Eventually he was dishonourably discharged from the army, but we never found out why. We think he engineered it.

Then, he met someone.

Someone very rich.

That someone said that she was building a new pier in the north, a super aquarium, a palace palladium and a brand new boardwalk.

This interested Edward Fear, because he saw potential in it for his own fame.

The person he met, the very rich person, soon became his wife, and the new North Pier was built, with Prophet Zaar as he was now officially known, as the face of the advertising campaign.

He consulted with his ball, with the undead.

Some say he traded the life of his first child, who was named Corrine, for the new North Pier to be a success.

Mind you, all of this is just rumour.

They say his real stroke of genius was masking his Happiness Machine with the smell of candyfloss.

Once he discovered how to do that, he let it work its magic.

By the time he stepped out onto the floor of the

Palace Palladium on a Saturday night, people would be riding high, peaking from clouds of The Happiness Machine that were seeping through the air vents.

Then, on the microphone, he'd launch into his spiel, one that every man, woman and child on the island knew by heart:

As man was born
By woman's womb,
In the eye of a
Drowning Moon
I'll be your guide,
Your happiness harpoon
All the things that I'll
Show you soon:

The burning tower,
The steeplechase
A girl that smiles
Without a face
I will show you
Ships upon a wave
And strange illusions that
You can't explain

The twisted hand,
The magic wheel
A tarot card
A devil's deal
I will show that
Wonders can be real
With these
Strange illusions that I
Will reveal

PROPHET ZAAR

LESS THAN NOTHING

They were putting out a bonfire this morning. Two men with waders on, stabbing at the ground with pitchforks. Smouldering wood littered the silver beach. I stood there for ages, just watching.

There was an Alsatian hot-footing over the glowing embers. It was like one of those religious rituals. The burning coal walk. And the transit van with the big rake tied to the back that belched blue smoke and nearly got stuck in the quicksand. They even launched the lifeboat tractor, until two pieces of driftwood gave enough traction for the tires. It was touch and go for an hour or so.

Should we have helped last night, on the sand that looked like a flooded oilfield? Should we have ran over, pulled at the legs and dragged it out of the fire? Was it a real person or a stuffed dummy? Penny for the guy, the kids say, with outstretched arms. I think they're hiding something. We'll never know.

It's evening now and I'm sitting in the dunes, looking at the promenade hotel. The glowing red of the sign, all joined up in double writing, like an old film poster. It bleeds the same colour as the chemical works in the distance. And Snake Mountain Rollercoaster making its final run of the night, as if in slow motion. The cold wind stings my cheeks.

I haven't done a thing all day. Nothing. Less than nothing, in fact. I had it planned for weeks. There's a note in my diary next to today's date. It says: WRITE-OFF. I write days off because it's my decision and nobody else's. I can send any of them to the scrapheap, Monday to Sunday. It's the only thing I have any real power over.

IT WASN'T ALWAYS LIKE THIS

When was nostalgia invented? I mean the first idea of life being somehow better in a past time, a distant glory-era. It must be a recent thing. It has to be.

Could have been the end of World War II. The way people came together like that. Or the birth of rock n' roll, possibly. When the first tremolo guitar and slap-back snare rattled through the radio. Pink tuxedos and bolo ties. Skiffle bands in railway stations. Teenagers talking in secret slang, all oilslicked and pale as ghosts. The heave of the fairground.

People walk around here like they're carrying the past on their shoulders. They won't leave it alone. They're drunk on sentimentality. They didn't lock their front doors in the old days, they say. There was no need. And the drug thing, it didn't exist. Now you've got kids climbing through kitchen windows, trying to steal your dog.

They sell picture postcards on the beachfront. Fat women in deckchairs who trade innuendos. Orangutans dressed up like pensioners, wearing rosettes and straw hats. Pantomime costumes. Teenagers stand outside chip shops and take photographs,

reimagining their lives as a Martin Parr negative.
I'm sick of the past just as much as I am of the pres-
ent. And what about the future?

Nostalgia is everywhere on the island. Faded album
sleeves get pinned to plasterboard pub walls. Broken
jukeboxes sit idle in dusty backrooms. They haven't
spun a record since the three-day week. Tommy
Dorsey. Billy Fury. The Big Three. Gerry and the
Pacemakers. They stare back at us like angry gods.

SNAKE MOUNTAIN ROLLERCOASTER

It's one thing to boast about it. Actually doing it takes some guts. It's the rejection that some fear and others feed off. The question: Can I take you on Snake Mountain? Boys ask girls and girls size them up with their eyes. After that they muddle away, arm-in-arm, to wait in a winding queue and watch the ride climb and drop and climb again over serpentine scaffold that touches the sky.

It begins in silence. NO STANDING. A gap between two bodies. Knuckles white around the safety-bar, the creak of wet wood in the wind. It happens slow, the ascent. A lurch of the stomach. As the car freezes at the peak, they look up and out:

The stars, collapsing.
The Moon iris, glowing.
A groan in the Earth's axis.
The distant hulk of frozen shipyards.
The sensation of dying, of being born, of being stuck in time.
The smell of candy floss and energy drinks, cheap drugs on the slow wind.
The gypsy kid with his apron on, staring up from the controls.

Then the vein popping thrust of gravity, eyes bulging out to the darkness, the trace of pier lights like sparklers, jaws wrenched shut in the click-jump. Loop the loop, around the bend, and spin back in. It ends as quickly as it begins.

They exit the ride together, dizzy, and stay that way, sometimes forever.

Where do the screams escape to?

SNAKE MOUNTAIN

CIRCUS DRIVERS

Even though we've been on the road with each other for the best part of twenty years, it still kills me to be around him when he eats. The way he picks at the plate like that. And the sound of him chewing, I can feel it in my spine, the fillings of my teeth. It's dread and irritation and disgust all rolled into one.

But after all, I'm aware that all he's really doing is eating, and I'm probably the one in the wrong. It can get that way when two people spend too much time together.

We speak at breakfast, usually, because he drives the nightshift, while I kip in a small bunk behind the front seat. I'll take the wheel at dawn, after whatever motorway servo we choose to eat at, and he'll curl up in the same spot.

He'll sleep a deep, uninterrupted sleep after rubbing speed into his gums right the way through the night, waking me up by having frenzied conversations with himself.

It's these vagaries of his personality that, when we eat together, make me want to roll up my Daily Mirror and stab it through his vampiric heart.

I remember a time when I could live through movies. I'd sit there in motorway hotels (when you could still rent movies from the in-room TV), and lie there for a day, or however long the company layover was, losing myself in films.

If there was a character that I could relate to in some way, I'd become it, wholly. Everything in my life would suddenly revolve around that actor. I'd see props and sets everywhere, even in the super mundane: road signs, the colour of a plastic chair in a waiting room, waitresses who looked like supporting actresses.

I'd fall in love too, easily in those days, because the heady magnetism of love and lust seem to increase whenever you're in transit. I can never explain why that is.

Later, I bought a laptop and began to stream old movies like *Days of Heaven* and *Five Easy Pieces*. Burt Lancaster really did a number on me, after that film *Elmer Gantry*. I pictured myself as the journeyman preacher, rolling into the backwoods of Britain in search of an old widow to con an inheritance out of.

In those days, when we worked non-stop, we were ghosts; in and out within four hours, usually. We could've got away with anything.

We came as a team, me and him, not through friendship, more through the fact we'd driven the breadth of Europe a million times over in a Leyland Daf, before being laid off.

These days, we go under the name of whatever opaque shell company we're hired by, no questions asked.

Mostly we work for Mr Bostock's Big Top of Wonder, which is a kind of travelling fair, owned by a man called Jono.

We drive the big tops around in huge trucks. The tents have to be loaded out and set up at night, because if anyone saw how unsafe those things are we'd be shut down in a heartbeat.

We go all around Coral Island, then sometimes over to Britain, if the work is there. Coral Islanders call Britain, where we come from, 'Rainland' and people who come from there 'Rainlanders."

We're paid well by Jono, I think because there's danger involved.

When the fair is shutting down, there'll be hundreds of people lifting, heaving packing, everyone helping out.

But when only the big tops remain, everyone disappears. The field will be brightly lit, and the final and most dangerous job is left to he and I, my driving partner.

One Christmas, we were driving to back to Coral Island.

We'd rolled off the night ferry and had a two-day layover not far from the North Pier, at the docks. It was below zero, and the blanket of frost added to the eerie sense of abandonment around there. It was freezing in the cab, too, even with the blowers turned up full.

The docks were pretty run down. You'd see all these big, beautiful empty warehouses. Huge shipping cranes left to rust, tyre fitting garages everywhere and a huge military destroyer with scaffold around it.

The hotel we stayed in was near this school. St. Elmo's Correction School, I remember it was called.

I was sleeping late that day. The kids must have been out on their first break, because I could half-hear them in the playground. I was dreaming about him, my travelling companion.

In the dream, he was about to commit murder. I was tracking him through a neighbourhood in Los Angeles. I must have been a detective, I think, because I'd watched *Eight Millimetre* with Nicolas Cage that night, and I was doing these weird Elvis kung-fu kicks, the way Cage used to do when he went on talk shows, even though I was meant to be working incognito. It was a pretty daft dream, if I'm honest.

I followed him for hours, until we reached a crowded shopping centre. I was hiding behind a fibreglass palm tree when I saw him reach into his jeans and pull out a huge machete, the type Michael Douglas cuts through the jungle with in *Romancing the Stone*.

Anyway, he starts picking people at random, hacking at them with the knife. I mean, really cutting them deep: an old couple in matching turquoise sweaters, two teenage twins on bikes, sunlight gleaming off their dental braces as they fall simultaneously from the saddles.

Blood everywhere.

And as I'm sleeping, the sound of the children laughing and shouting outside in the playground merged with the dream of this man tearing through an American retail park.

That day, I stayed in my room until noon. I sloped out of a fire exit at the back of the hotel and walked along a dock road until I came to a McDonald's.

The golden arches had been wrapped in tinsel and somebody had gifted Ronald McDonald an empty bottle of Bell's.

They'd removed his head, too, and replaced it with one of The Coral.

They've got their own statues out there on the North Pier. Anyway, Ronald's head was now one of the Pauls: Molloy, or Duffy.

I placed my order and ate alone, acting out odd kung-fu moves under the table between mouthfuls.

HOLES

I won't dig holes for him anymore. Why? Because my back hurts. The welts on my palms are beginning to weep. I'm waist deep in sand and silt while he lounges in a deckchair and smokes Mayfairs. It's not fair.

The same question keeps presenting itself: What are we digging for? Not for money. Not for bodies. Not for drugs. Not for fossils. Not for weapons. Not for diamonds. Not for coal. Not for-the-good-of-our-health. Not for God. What are we digging for? I never get an answer. I ask him again, heave my upper body up to where his bare feet rest on the sand. He folds up his newspaper and looks out, beyond me, toward the pale water of Coral Island.

"Get it done," he says. "Then we can go and eat."

LOCAL FOCUS

They edit footage of the South Pier to make it look worse than it is. You see it in everything: news reports, documentaries, CCTV footage. There's somebody working behind the scenes to blacken its name. You'll hear about a gang fight that might or might not have happened, a ballroom that's been condemned because the ceiling caved in, or a legendary fish bar closing down because somebody decided they didn't have the right food hygiene certificate.

In contrast to that, there's the North Pier. Their propaganda machine is relentless. They must have a Hollywood budget up there. Everything you see or hear about it is positive. A couple who got married on the boardwalk, a kid who's dying wish is to meet the strongman Mike Titanic, a girl who pulled a real emerald from a teddy picker. You know they covered up a murder out there, out near the pony rides and flea market? Did you know that?

The North Pier's so consuming, it sucks life out of the rest of the island. It's like Disney, all spit and polished on the outside, but with a hidden heart of darkness. Like there's some puppet master pulling the strings, brainwashing us all. I'll admit: it's hard not to have a good time when you're there. You can lose yourself for days in the mirror mazes and underground Laser Quest tunnels. But it's as if they're trying to make it a movie, or a dream. Something that looks real but isn't, like an illusion.

THE CORAL ISLAND
STEEPLECHASE DISASTER

I dreamed my first wicker man.

In the dream, everything was burning: houses, trees, even the sea. Fish were flopping onto the beach to get out of the boiling water.

I was walking through the flames.

It was me, only me, who the fire couldn't harm.

I rescued some birds from a tree, a field mouse and a small cat that was hiding in a Biffa bin.

I tucked them under my arms and into my pockets and told them I was here to save them, and that they should trust me, which they did.

Get to a high place, I thought.

The highest point was the top of a hill where this huge wicker man stood. It was pointing down at me with one hand. With his other hand, he held a huge staff.

Then the flames began to burn.

Slowly at first, but soon I could feel them charring my skin into whelps and blisters.

The floor beneath me became quicksand. I couldn't walk.

From under my jacket, I heard the cat meow. The field mouse squealed and the birds squawked.

I called out to the wicker man. I said, "Now, now. Do it now because this is the big scene. Do it!"

The wicker man in my dream, he heard me.

His big, free hand moved down and scooped me up. The animals were grateful. I felt like I was their true mother, and the wicker man was their father.

We sat in his belly and watched the land burn through the smoke and the cinders.

When I woke up, my fingernails were black with soot. There were two birds, a cat, and a field mouse on the windowsill outside my bedroom.

Each of them looked at me before they scattered.

We all knew.

That was my first wicker man, and wasn't my last. After I had the dream, I began building them.

Firstly, you have to make a frame. A few nails a ladder and a saw will do it.

Build it good and strong and talk it through its birth.

"There, there. Shhhh."

Decide what you want it to look like.

It can be anything: a horned goat-god, a sleep-walking Golem, a forest demon.

From then on it's about collecting hazel, willow withies, or honeysuckle vine, and bending them into the framework to form a basic human shape.

Make it up as you go. If you believe in him, he'll come alive.

Some of the wicker men I've built have been used in movies. Some are used on the shoreline of Estrangia, supposedly to guard against the evils of Rainland.

Once I was commissioned to build three wicker men to go around a horseracing track.

On Coral Island, a wicker man can be a symbol of luck, as well as protection.

I made three brothers.

One was The Gift of Wisdom, one was The Gift of Chance and one was the Gift of Fortune.

I made the brothers so big that they ring-a-rosed around the whole racetrack.

Betting is big business on the South Pier, and any kind of meet draws a big crowd. The day the track opened, it was the first time people had seen my wicker men.

It was a hot day, blisteringly hot. Horses were being hosed down in the paddocks because one or two had fainted.

But outside it was cooler, and people were coming up and hugging me with tears in their eyes. They couldn't believe what I'd built.

As the day went on, the temperature rose.

In the stables, a couple of hay bales had started to smoke. On the main concourse, plastic seating panels warped and sagged.

People were going down with heatstroke.

When the main race started I began to get that feeling again, the one I had in the dream, where everything was burning.

I saw it first.

The wicker man I called The Gift of Chance caught fire at his Achilles. It went up and spread to his arm, which was inexorably linked to his brother, The Gift of Fortune. The Gift of Fortune was linked to The Gift of Wisdom and back to The Gift of Chance.

Before long, they were a raging inferno.

My first thought was to run to the stables. I unlatched all the doors, setting the horses free. Most of them bolted onto the Fall Fields and galloped up toward Finniland, where they were eventually rounded up.

The horses and people on the racetrack didn't fare so well.

They said smoke inhalation caused most of the fatalities. They had to bring in JCB diggers to clear the bodies of the biggest thoroughbreds.

It became known as the Coral Island Steeplechase Disaster, and I never got over it.

I stopped dreaming of, and building, wicker men after that.

LAST NIGHT
OF THE HOLIDAYS

It ends the same way it began: A backseat dream down miles of winding hedgerows, our dad steering the car around ravine dirt roads and valley bluffs, the lurch and veer of the car as loose sandstone cracks and plunges five thousand fathoms deep below us into a blue sea. The white-hot fear of everybody except our driver.

As we lunge forward I start to notice a poster stapled to telegraph poles: SCOTT MAY'S DAREDEVIL SHOW. A photograph of a monster truck wheelieing over a ramp of wrecked cars. We stop at a junction and I read one: Car and fire stunts! Freestyle motocross! Clowning! Westway Camp Site, Caravan City! It flaps in the breeze as we pass.

Everybody silent now as we dawdle down a sloping cinder path. It funnels us to a rocky outcrop where everything opens up; a banquet of lights and Ferris wheels, spots of blurred electricity like will o' the wisp. Above us, a sky of indigo mystery. We crane our necks to take it in. Somebody says, "Eyes on the road."

I see it in the distance as we approach; the temporary grandstand, rickety and rocking in the breeze, the whole skeleton of it like an ancient pantheon, its wire frame like matchsticks. Surrounding it, mounds of earth have been bulldozed into ramps. Scrambler bikes somersault through the bluewheeze of exhaust smoke. Everything happens at once.

Where to go after this? What life to return to? The house, the street I knew has vanished into figments, a memory puzzle. Some of the pieces are missing. I hear my name and expect someone else to answer. I roll the window down and feel the wind in my hair, smells and sounds that acquiesce into the underbelly of my imagination, the place where dreams are stored. I close my eyes and it occurs to me that I'd never seen the sea until a week ago.

I'd never seen the sea.

THE LIGHT
THE DEAD SEE

You can see the dead at night, when the sea freighters draw toward the bay in the chop and riptide and their sidelights blink under the water.

The lights reflect off the lantern of a sunken lightship called The Arklow.

A lightship is a ship that acts as a lighthouse where one can't be built, because of rocks or deep water.

Because of the rocks off Coral Island, The Arklow was docked there in 1907. It sank in 1952 when its spurring wheel let the anchor chain out too fast.

It went up in flames from the surge of heat.

You hear this kind of story in the bars along Bungalow Bay where the old fishermen go.

So these days, when the big ships come in bringing their goods- counterfeit scratch cards, one armed bandits, arcade machines and dodgem shells- The Arklow lights up again, temporarily, on the sea bed. And that's when we see the dead.

They can be seen hovering around the water, just above the rocks.

We call them Faceless Angels.

It's only us who know about the dead, or the Faceless Angels.

We lie there at the cliff edge on our bellies looking down. They're locked in a kind of ritual dance, illuminated by the opaline glare of the wreck of The Arklow.

We know who some of the dead are:

Ryan and Robbie Quinn, who raced a stolen car around the island, flipped it, and ploughed headfirst over the bluffs, the radiator grill shattering every tooth in their twinned mouths so that they had to be identified by tattoos on their knuckles.

Eleanor Seagraves, who died heartbroken after an online romance with a nineteen stone conman pretending to be a French poet.

The Fitzgibbon widow, too, who simply walked into the sea.

Leo Gaskill, full of holes.

The unnamed man who climbed onto the spine of Snake Mountain, the frozen rollercoaster on Coral Bay, toward the frightened and trapped children, then fell to his own death after they had been saved.

The victims of the Coral Island Steeplechase Disaster.

There are more dead, but these are the dead we recognise.

Sometimes if the sea is calm you can hear them whisper:

Ring-a-ring-a-roses-a-pocketful-of-posies-a-tissue-a-tissue-we-all-fall-down.

It's a fleeting moment and you have to be quick, or you'll miss it.

At home, if one of us happens to see a freighter in the bay, we run to each other's houses, up and down the cobbled streets, shouting at each other to come out.

On the cliff edge, we'll line up again, stretched out on our bellies, and watch. It's like a performance.

The light from the big ships is the light we see, and the glare coming from the sunken Arklow is the light the dead see.

WHY THE ARKLOW CAUGHT FIRE AT CORAL BAY

"Well, it caught fire because they lost anchor. They lost anchor simply because the fella behind the windlass - you could see him continually releasing the brakewheel instead of waiting for tension on the anchor cable to spool out more chain - and by the time enough tension had accumulated, the brake was so wide open it was unable to slow down the spinning gypsy, or the chainwheel if you prefer. The brake pads didn't cope very well, and disintegrated in no time.

I dropped anchors with the same size chain when I was the bosun on a few ships, and never would we release a brake beyond a few turns for fear that something like that would happen. No chance. Anyway the sparks from the friction set the wooden hull alight.

Before the fire, the worst thing that happened to me was getting rust chips embedded in my eye from the chain coming out of the spurring pipe at high speed... I wasn't wearing goggles. The chips had to be surgically removed and I was blind all the way through Christmas."

LAST NIGHT
OF THE FAIR

I am running on the balls of my feet in the pitch dark.

I am frightened.

My legs are silly putty.

My mouth tastes of metal.

I am pegging it.

Full blast.

Earlier, the night had been lit, a tapestry of neon brilliance. Connie and me, we soaked up the North Pier until we were drunk on teddy pickers and water guns and whack-a-mole games.

I stole a bag of turquoise candyfloss and we ate it under the holy glow of a wonder wheel. After that we were supercharged.

We laughed at a friend of Jono's called Crayford. He was skulking about the shooting booths. He looked too old to be there, sad that his friends had grown up and reneged on the sacred pact of child-hood.

Well, I thought, that would never happen to me and Connie.

We weren't growing up, not ever, and that was that.

Under the Snake Mountain rollercoaster, we

played Paper, Scissors, Rock and I let him win
because I always let Connie win except when it's for
control of the telly.

Connie wins again.

He took the last bluey from my hand and went in
the queue.

You might ask where we got that kind of money.

Well.

Before we went out we said Jono Jono give us some
slummy for the rides. Give us some slummy for the
rides, Jon.

I'll take you down he said.

Our fair had packed down by then so we were
going up to the North Pier promenade.

It's the last night of our stay on Coral Island
before we go on a six-month tour of Rainland.

When Jono said he'll take us down our hearts sank
because he'd sat there with a cob on for a week.

His snooker cue was broke and Tammy was somewhere else. He was down on his luck.

I'll take you down, Jono said.

You don't have to Jono.

We'll be alright.

Yeah Jono, we're alright.

Get my leather. The one with the fur collar.

As it happened, Jono was in a generous mood.

We got to the North Pier and he pulls a ten-spot
and two blueys out of his pocket, and hands them to
me.

That's twenty quid.

Go on, he said.

So I'm stood there watching Connie about to ride Snake Mountain's final circuit of the night.

What it does is, it trundles along slow at first. It takes you up the curve of its back before hurtling headfirst into the abyss, around a breakneck curve then a full loop the loop. But that's just while it gets warmed up before it goes into hyperspeed.

Connie was in the front car, alone. I could make out the hood on his windbreaker and the little bald patch in his hair where I'd nicked him in a clipper fight. He kept looking back as if to say, can you believe it, can you believe I won again.

It trundled up and stopped at the peak.

And I knew as soon as it gave itself to gravity it was moving too quick or too wrong or too something.

It sprang forward like a lurcher almost like it was falling down the stairs drunk.

The sheer force took it round the loop the loop once, twice, a hundred times like some human wheel of fortune, and I could see Connie's face pressed forward to the wind.

His eyes were big and his face had no sound.

I'll never forget the screech of the brakes, they were like wailing banshees, the death messengers dad told us about.

A great sea of sparks flew and it ground to a halt.

Connie was stuck there, upside down at the top of Snake Mountain with five or six others.

He looked me dead in the eye and I nodded.

Jono.

I run back, back to the boardwalk where he left us.

He is still there, glowing under a halo light.

Before he can hear me he's seen the whites of my eyes and his beer plunges to the floor with a tremendous GLUNK.

Tammy is there. She pulls at the spilled beer froth at the tips of her curls and shakes it from her fingertips.

Already he's moving.

He's leapt over a moving carousel. He darts toward me like a hungry angel, the silhouette of him terrific and headfirst in the luminous brume and for a crazy second I forget about Connie.

Here.

Here he is.

And I'm shouting with blood in my throat Jono Jono Jono come quick.

Jono come on.

LAST NIGHT OF THE FAIR

THE END